SHARK 1

CATHERINE BANKS

TURBO KITTEN

Shark 1 by Catherine Banks.

Copyright © 2022 Catherine Banks

Cover design and graphic art by JoY Author Design.

Published by Turbo Kitten Industries.

www.CatherineBanks.com

Turbo Kitten Industries™, P.O. Box 5012, Galt, CA 95632

Thank you to my amazing husband who continues to support me. I love you and your amazing cuddles.

PREFACE

This was first published on Vella, so you may notice that these chapters are shorter than my normal ones. That is due to the episodic format. Don't worry, this is the complete first book, but be warned you may zoom through it with chapters being shorter.

Happy reading! :)

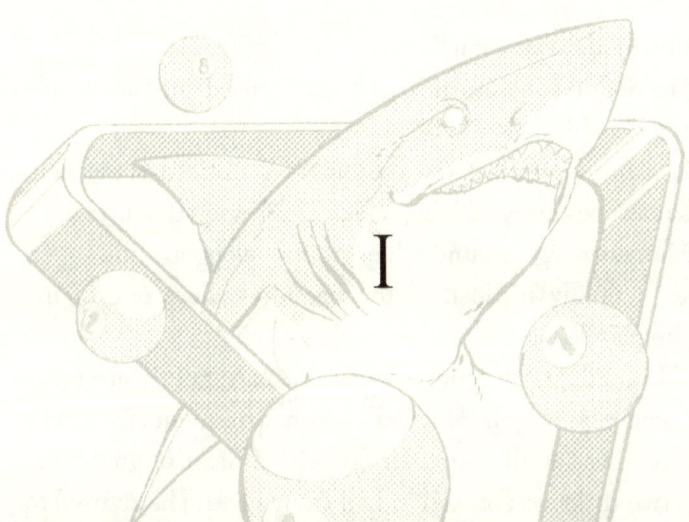

I

The cacophony of voices mixed with bass-filled music drew me like a siren luring a sailor into the water. The bar was busier than usual, even for a Friday night, thanks to the holiday on the upcoming Monday, but that was perfect. It meant lots of new, gullible idiots, which meant more money in my pocket.

I stepped into the bar with my mouth closed to hide my teeth out of habit.

"Welcome back, Kass," Tonka, the bouncer manning the door greeted me with a smile. He had to stand to the side of the doorway, or no one would get in because of his formidable size. The half-troll, half-orc was huge and took no crap from anyone.

"Hey, Tonka," I replied, and gave him a small smile, careful not to show too much of my teeth, or he'd take it as a threat. Trolls were highly volatile and got into fights often for mistaking body language as a threat.

"You let me know if anyone gives you trouble tonight, okay?" he insisted.

I nodded. "You got it."

He nodded in return, and then focused on the people coming in behind me.

Looking around at the customers, I noticed some delicious new eye candy. "Hello, sexies," I whispered to myself.

Maneuvering around the groups clogging the open spaces, I finally made it to the bar top, where one of my favorite people was.

"Hey, Silver," I called to get the bartender's attention from where he was chatting with another frequent customer.

Silver was a tall, muscular orc with a heart of gold. One of his two tusks was broken in half from a battle he refused to talk about. He'd put a piercing through the broken tusk and the piece of jewelry glittered in the lights as he turned to face me. The smile he'd had grew wider when he saw me, and he hurried down the bar to stand before me. "Kassidy, I had hoped to get to see you tonight."

He was the only one who used my full name, even after knowing me for several years.

"You know I wouldn't miss a Friday night," I replied, smiling wide at him.

The human man sitting on the barstool to my right flinched when he saw my triangular, serrated shark teeth.

"Come to the office for a second," Silver said, his smile slipping a bit as he said it.

Uh oh. This was not good. He never pulled me off to the side to chat, except that one time I'd taken every dollar a guy had on him during a pool match, and the guy had gone to Silver crying about not being able to pay his drinking bill.

"Sure," I agreed, and headed around to the side of the long wooden bar.

Once on the side, he stepped out to meet me, bent down so his head was beside mine, and whispered, "Hunters are in town and are supposed to come by tonight. Behave, so I don't have to fix my bar."

My eyes widened and I let my mouth drop open. "I am offended! I would never destroy your bar."

He smirked. "I know you wouldn't, but you wouldn't hesitate to piss off someone and they'd trash my place trying to hurt you. I don't feel like buying more furniture, and I'm getting old and tired of fighting."

"You're not old," I said and rolled my eyes. "And you have bouncers working here to do that for you."

"Did you know that my bouncers take your safety into consideration even before a human's? I've tried telling them your skin is tougher than even mine, but they won't listen. Let's not test their loyalty to you over the humans who are visiting tonight," he said, and gave me a stern glare.

I patted his arm and smiled. "You got it, boss! Best behavior."

He snorted and shook his head. "I don't know why I bother. You're going to do whatever you want anyway."

"Oh my gosh, it's almost like you know her," the voice of my best friend said from down the bar.

I peeked around the tall guys beside me, spotting her leaning against the middle of the bar beside an empty stool. "Theo!" I yelled and ran to her, throwing my arms around her shoulders. She wore a long rainbow skirt with a bright pink crop top that showed off her super toned abs. Today she wore a wig that was long, silver colored, and complimented her stormy gray eyes, making them look ethereal.

She hugged me back and whispered, "What did the old orc want to talk to you about?"

"Hunters are in town, and he thinks they're going to come here," I advised her, because she needed to know, too.

Theo pulled back and scowled. "Seriously? Ugh. I hate hunters." Theo had a long history with hunters that almost always ended with their bodies strewn about the beach.

"Silver said we have to behave in the bar," I told her.

She chuckled. "I'll try to keep you in line."

I scoffed. "It's you who is going to have to be kept in line. I don't hate hunters, they hate me."

She rolled her eyes, turned to face Silver, who was back behind the bar, and said, "Our usual, please." She batted her eyelashes at him while smiling wide.

Silver said, "No."

Theo and I stared at him in disbelief. Had the old orc just told us no? He never said no.

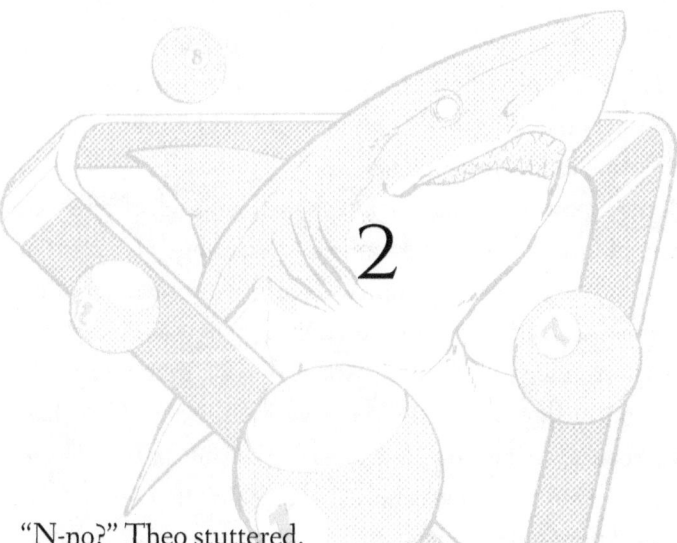

2

"N-no?" Theo stuttered.

Laughter boomed out of him so loudly that everyone in the bar turned to look. He bent over, clutching at his stomach as he continued to laugh. "Your f-faces!" More laughter followed and didn't stop until tears streamed down his face.

"Did I break him?" I asked softly to Theo.

"You do have a habit of breaking men," Theo agreed while still staring at Silver, wide-eyed.

Silver straightened and wiped his eyes. "Sorry, loves. I just had to see what would happen. My answer is still no, but only because I want you to try something new tonight."

Theo glared at him and put her hands on her narrow hips. "You could have just said that."

"Well, whip it out," I said, with a wide smile at Silver.

His eyes narrowed and he growled softly before turning around to start making the drinks. He hated when I made sexual innuendos to him, since he viewed me as a pseudo daughter.

"How was work?" I asked Theo, turning my back to the bar, so I could look out at the crowd while also looking at her.

She sighed and flipped her hair over her shoulder. "Three people came in looking for a love spell. Morons."

Being a powerful mage meant she got her pick of jobs, but because of a rough past, she took easy jobs now. Her current position was one she'd kept for two years, working at a potion shop making potions and stockpiling ingredients. Love potions were illegal and didn't work anyway, they just made the person enslaved to whoever gave it to them. Theo had been forced to drink one, and it had taken her a full day to break free. That person was never seen again.

"You know what you need?" I asked with a mischievous smile. "Dancing!"

She sighed and shook her head. "You always say dancing."

"Because you love it!" I shouted.

"Here," Silver said.

We turned and I gasped at the sparkly, swirling teal drink. "You got the edible drink glitter!" I'd told him about the stuff a month ago and he'd scoffed and told me he wouldn't buy crap like that.

"Well, apparently it's popular and women are more likely to order additional drinks if they can get sparkly ones. You are worse than dragons with your shiny obsession," he grumbled.

I picked the martini glass up carefully, watching the spinning glitter. "How did you get the drink to be such a bright teal?" I asked.

Theo said, "Magic. It's infused with a little power-up that

I make." She arched a brow at Silver. "Why didn't you ask me to get this for you? I can give you a discount."

"I don't give you drink discounts, so I don't want discounts from you," he said, crossing his arms over his chest.

He was such a proud orc.

"Cheers," I said, holding my glass up towards Theo.

She picked hers up and clinked it against mine. "Cheers!"

Normally, we chugged our first drink, but this time we took a small drink to taste it.

It tasted like mangoes! My favorite fruit ever.

"Why are you spoiling her?" Theo asked as she took another drink. "This is delicious, by the way."

"I'm not spoiling her," he muttered, turning away to wipe down the counter that was sparkling clean.

I smiled smugly and Theo rolled her eyes.

"Spoiled brat," she whispered.

"You love the drink, too," I countered as she took a larger gulp.

We finished our drinks at the same time.

I grabbed her hand and pulled her through the bar area, up the stairs, and to the dance floor, which was only half-full at the moment.

Once in the center, I released her hand and started swaying to the beat.

She danced in front of me, more graceful than I could ever be, and instantly became the center of attention.

Theo shone like a diamond, no matter what she wore, and I smiled happily to see it. There had been a time when Theo had been surrounded by darkness, when she hadn't accepted who she truly was. Seeing the darkness gone made my heart soar for my bestie. She deserved happiness and to be her true self. Everyone did.

As we danced, the bar filled up, and Theo leaned close to whisper, "Easy targets at six o'clock."

I smiled, spun on my heel while still dancing in front of her, and spotted the college guys easily. Oh, yeah. They were going to pay for our drinks tonight.

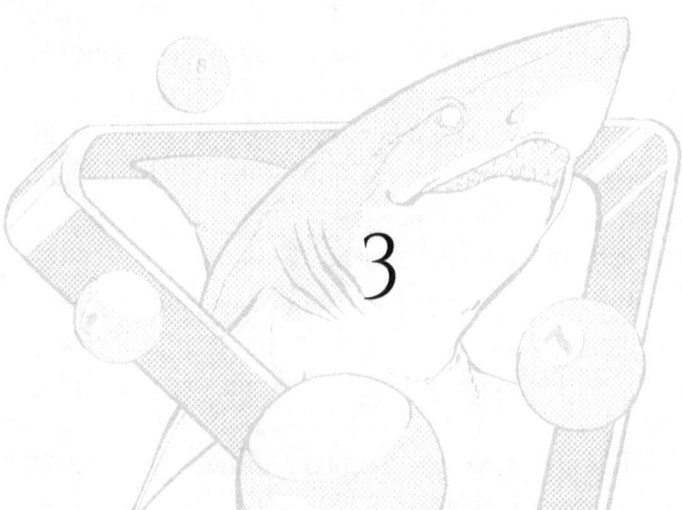

3

After a few more swings of my hips, I spun back around and yelled louder than needed, "Let's get a drink and then I want to try playing pool! It looks fun!"

Theo rolled her eyes, but followed me downstairs, back to Silver.

"One minute," he told us gruffly, as he grabbed a few bottles out from under the bar.

"They take the bait?" I asked out the side of my mouth and tapped my fingers to the beat atop the wooden bar top.

She nodded while watching Silver. "They headed to the tables."

Oh, they were falling right into our trap. Perfect.

"Excuse me," a deep male voice said beside me.

I turned and realized I was leaning half over an open barstool. "Oh, my bad. Sorry," I said and moved closer to Theo.

The guy sat on the stool and smiled at me. "No problem." He was averagely handsome, had a scar over his left eye, and I felt the pressure of a predator from him. Though it seemed he was trying to rein in the predator aura, not an easy task.

Beside him were three other newcomers. Two were twins that looked like models and the third was possibly the most handsome man I had ever seen.

"You guys on vacation?" I asked.

The twins looked up with narrowed eyes and then looked away simultaneously.

"Sort of," the super handsome one on the end replied with a soft smile.

"Well, if you want the best pizza in town, go to Gina's two blocks north," I told them.

"Kassidy," Silver said to get my attention.

I turned and picked up the drink he'd set down. "Thank you, Silver."

"Oh, I want that," the guy beside me said.

"You want that drink?" Silver asked. "The sparkly drink?"

He nodded. "It looks like it tastes delicious."

"It does," I said and took a drink. "So delicious."

"I like seeing a man who isn't afraid to drink something sparkly," Theo said as she stepped out from beside me.

The guy smiled at her and said, "Shiny things are a weakness of mine."

I stared at the group of guys as they placed their orders. Something about them was ... different. They weren't all the same race, and yet they seemed like a team. Were they best friends?

"Kass, pool?" Theo asked.

"Oh, right," I said and tore my eyes away from the guys.

"See you around," the hot guy said with a smile.

I returned his smile as I was rudely pulled away by my cock-blocking bestie.

"Only if you're lucky," Theo said with a wink, before my view was blocked by a group of vampires standing around a table.

"Things were just getting interesting," I whined.

She shook her head. "Let's get our drinking money first. Then you can flirt with the shapeshifters."

"Were they all shapeshifters?" I asked. Theo could use a spell to see what type of magic someone had. She couldn't tell what kind of shapeshifter they were, but she would see their shapeshifter magic.

"I couldn't tell with the twins. They had shields around even their auras," she whispered. "Super weird."

We stepped into the next room where a dozen pool tables were set up. All of them were taken, but I spotted the college guys at one.

"Should we pout, or is that too obvious?" I asked softly, and leaned against the wall.

"No pouting," Theo said with a wide smile. She sighed dramatically. "Oh, man, the tables are all taken." She'd said it loud enough the entire room had heard.

"I wanted to try playing pool," I whined. "Maybe one will open up soon."

She sighed and dropped her head to take a long drink.

"You think I can do that splitting thing?" I asked.

"Breaking," Theo corrected.

"Right, that," I said with a ditzy smile that hid my teeth.

On cue, two of the four college boys walked over to us.

"Hey," the one with perfectly straight, white teeth greeted us.

"Hi," I said softly.

"You ladies like to play a game? We've played pool together too many times, and it's boring playing against each other," he said.

"We've never played before," Theo commented. "You'd have to teach us the rules."

The second guy, dark and handsome, smiled and said, "We'll gladly teach you beautiful ladies. What are your names?"

"I'm Theo," she said breathlessly.

"Kassidy," I answered as I stared up at Mr. Perfect Teeth, batting my eyelashes like a lost little puppy. "If you're sure you don't mind," I said and headed towards their table.

Two of the usual customers looked up from their pool game and snickered.

I gave them a glare and they returned to their game, still chuckling.

We made it to the other guys, who were sitting on two of the stools that lined the walls.

"This is Theo and Kassidy," Mr. Perfect Teeth introduced.

"We don't know your names yet," Theo reminded him.

He chuckled. "Where are my manners?"

A prickling sensation on the back of my neck made me angle my body slightly, so I could look back at the door.

The four hot guys from a minute ago walked in and out of pure luck snagged an open table.

"Did you want to try to break, or do you want me to do it?" Mr. Perfect Teeth, who I totally hadn't heard do introductions, said.

"Um, what's breaking?" I asked and twirled my hair around my finger.

"When you hit the first time into the group of balls," he explained patiently.

"Why don't you show me?" I suggested with a smile. "That way I can learn from example."

He nodded and moved around the table confidently, grabbed a cue from the wall, and lined up his shot.

I hadn't even noticed them rack it up. I did notice his form was awful and he didn't have the right hold on the stick, though.

"You alright?" Theo asked me softly.

I nodded. "Yeah. Yeah." I kept sneaking looks in the direction of the foursome, the hair on my nape still tingling.

"Focus for ten minutes," Theo ordered me. "Then you can flirt to your heart's content." She turned back to Mr. Dark and Delicious, amping up her flirting to ten.

4

When Perfect Teeth hit the ball, it barely staggered the balls, but I still gasped and smiled behind my hands.

"Now what?" I asked.

"Now, you use the stick to hit the ball, trying to get one of them into the pocket. Not the eight ball, though. If you get one in, whatever type of ball it is will be the one you're assigned," he explained.

I nodded emphatically, walked around the table, took the cue from him, and bent over, so my assets were on display in my tight jeans. "Like this?" I asked.

"Exactly like that," he said in a strained voice behind me.

"Wait, let's make a bet!" Theo said. "That'll make it more fun and we'll try harder."

"We don't want to take your money," Dark and Delicious said.

"Oh, it's fine. I've got Daddy's money burning a hole in my pocket anyway," I lied.

"You sure?" Perfect Teeth asked.

I nodded. "I always perform better when there's money on the table," I said, completely letting the innuendo stand.

Perfect Teeth turned around and grunted softly.

I pulled out a wad of cash from my pocket that was really a single hundred with a dozen ones inside of it. "What do you say we bet one hundred?" I asked.

They eyed the stack of money hungrily and looked at each other, communicating with looks alone.

Perfect Teeth took out some cash from his wallet, as did Dark and Delicious, splitting the cost.

"She's paying for me," Theo said. "The perks of having a rich bestie."

"Alright, whoever wins the match gets the two hundred dollars," Perfect Teeth said.

I held out my hand. "Agreed."

He shook my hand and I smiled wide, letting him see my teeth for the first time. His face paled noticeably, but he quickly recovered and returned my smile.

I bent back over the table, lined up my shot, and hit the cue ball.

Three solid-colored balls rolled into different pockets with ease.

I straightened and giggled. "That's easier than it looks."

"My turn!" Theo said, took the cue stick from me, and nudged me out of the way. "Could you help me?" she asked Dark and Delicious.

He shook his head to clear the stupor he'd been in after my shot, smiled and pressed up against her entire back. "Bend over and put your hands here," he instructed.

Theo kept as much of her touching him as she could while having horrible form. "Like this?"

"Must have been beginner's luck," Perfect Teeth whispered to one of his friends behind me.

"Totally. All the balls were on the table, so it was easy to knock a few in," his friend said.

I resisted the urge to roll my eyes, which just made my eyes roam towards the table of the foursome.

They were playing with serious expressions and rigid bodies. The longer I watched them, the stranger their body language became. Were they waiting for someone? People sometimes came to Silver's to meet with enemies, because Silver's was a neutral area.

"Oh, shoot!" Theo muttered as she straightened. "I didn't hit a single one."

She came over to me and I patted her arm with a smile. "I'm sure you'll hit one next time."

The guys took their turns, only sinking one ball each before it was finally my turn again.

I was bent over the table when I felt the aura of darkness enter the room.

Every non-human's head raised, sensing it, too, and searched for the source.

Just inside the room stood two men, wearing slacks and button-up shirts. They both had long black hair, braided down their backs, slightly pointed ears, and swirling black auras.

The hunters had arrived.

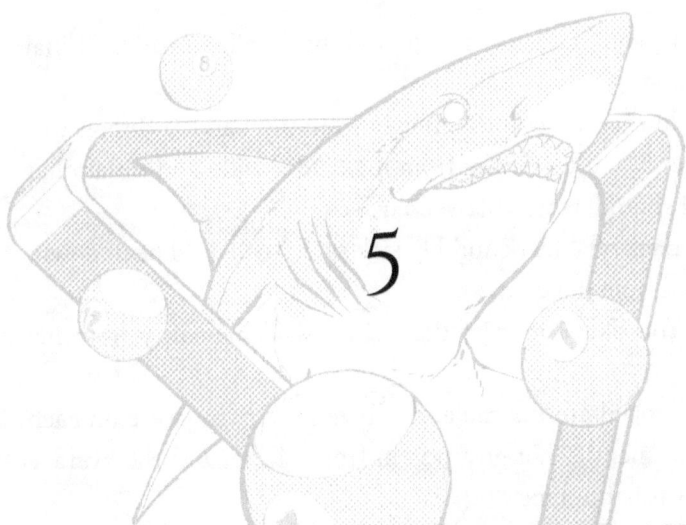

5

"Shit, time to wrap things up," I said as I noticed Theo's frozen body. With one final hit, I smoothly sank all of my balls and the eight ball into pockets. I snagged the two hundred dollars from atop the table and saluted the college guys. "Thanks for playing."

"Back door?" Theo asked.

"We could try walking past them," I suggested.

"Hey! You totally played us!" Perfect Teeth growled.

I looked over my shoulder at him and winked while smiling wide, so they could all see my teeth. "Yep! Thanks for the drinking money, boys. Feel free to come back again."

Theo headed towards the back door, head down, even though that did nothing to hide her bright wig and outfit.

I followed after her, but Dark and Delicious grabbed my bicep and jerked me to a stop. "Give us our money back."

I snarled at him. "Let go of me right now, or you'll lose that hand."

He squeezed harder. "Give us back our money." The skin on his face moved, betraying he was a shapeshifter.

"I won it. Suck it up and back off," I said. "Final warning."

He tried to grab the money from my hand and then was suddenly ten feet away from me, and a wide and unfamiliar set of shoulders was between us.

"Back off," Dark and Dickish said. Yeah, he'd been downgraded from delicious.

"You okay?" one of the twins asked me softly from my left.

I looked around me and realized the twins were on each side of me, the hot guy was in front of me, and the average guy was behind me.

Whoa, they were protecting me.

"I'm good," I assured them. "My skin's tough, so his pathetic grip didn't even leave a red spot."

"She's a pool shark," Dark and Dickish said.

Technically, I was also a shark, but I wasn't going to correct him.

Theo stood by the back door and I motioned her to leave with my hand. I could handle this, and she needed to get away from the hunters.

"This isn't your fight, Captain Save-A-Hoe," Dark and Dickish said.

"You're really so pathetic that you can't take that you got played by a hot chick?" Hot Guy asked.

He thought I was hot? I mean, I knew I was attractive, but hot was a tad over the top.

The three other college guys stepped forward and their upper bodies shifted, revealing tiger stripes.

Tiger shifters? I thought they were all hidden in some faraway place, since there were so few of them.

Hot Guy chuckled. "Morons."

The hunters ran forward and started fighting with the tiger shifters.

"Let's get out of here while they're distracted," Average Guy said.

They turned to leave, but stopped when I didn't follow.

Average Guy grabbed my hand and tugged. "Come on, Smiley."

Smiley?

The foursome walked out the back door that Theo had taken and out into the cool night air.

"You okay?" Tonka asked, pushing off the wall of the building and stamping out his cigarette, obviously on break.

"I'm good," I said. "The hunters are fighting some tiger shifters inside, though. So, you may want to go break that up."

He narrowed his eyes. "What did you do?"

"I didn't do anything, Tonka!" I shouted.

He sighed, opened the door, and muttered, "Damn sea-dweller."

"I heard that, you mountain oaf!" I shouted just before the door closed.

"Hungry?" one of the twins asked me.

"Um, yes," I replied, surprised by the sudden topic shift. "I'm Kassidy, but you can call me Kass."

The twins bowed their heads slightly. They were hard to tell apart, but the one on the left had a slightly brighter green around his eyes than the one on the right.

"I'm Jong-min and this is my younger brother Jong-hyun," the one on the left introduced.

"Nice to meet you, Min and Hyun," I said with a soft smile.

Jong-Min scowled and sternly said, "You do not have permission to address us so informally. Please refer to us by our correct names."

My smile slipped and I bowed my head slightly. "I'm sorry. I meant no offense."

They both nodded and I looked at Average Guy expectantly. Now that I was closer to him and under the moonlight, something about him seemed more attractive. Or maybe that was just my crazy brain.

"I'm Grant," he introduced.

"Reed," the last one, the hot one, said.

"Let's go get some food," Jong-min said. "I'm starving."

"What kind of food do you want?" I asked. "I'm really familiar with this town so I know all the best spots."

"How long have you lived here?" Grant asked.

"I've lived here a few years now." I did not want to explain that I didn't have an actual house or apartment here since I spent a lot of my time in shark form at the aquarium. They paid me really well to swim around one of their tanks for visitors during the day. Plus, I got free food and free housing out of the deal.

"We were thinking pizza, since you suggested that place," Reed said.

"Oh, you're going to love it. Gina's pizzas are the best," I said, and started towards the sidewalk.

They quickly caught up to me, with the twins walking on each side of me again, and the other two behind us.

"So, is pool hustling something you do often?" Jong-hyun asked.

I shrugged. "It pays well, and there are always people on vacation that visit Silver's bar."

"You seem to be a frequent customer," Jong-hyun commented.

"I like Silver's. It's got everything a girl could want for a night out: drinks, dancing, pool, and gullible guys." I smiled wide and chuckled.

"I like her," Grant said.

"How long are you boys in town?" I asked and turned around, walking backwards so I could look at all of them.

"That's classified," Jong-min snapped.

I shrugged. "Okay. How about you tell me what your favorite pizza toppings are then?"

"Meat combination," Reed answered.

"Vegetarian," Jong-min said.

Grant shrugged. "I eat whatever."

I looked at Jong-hyun, who fidgeted a moment before saying, "Same as my brother."

"Well, we should definitely get multiple pizzas, then. I mean, I'm sure you four eat more than a large pizza anyways." I chuckled after I said it and they all smiled, the tension easing even more.

My phone rang and I pulled it from my back pocket. I'd lucked out in getting a phone that folded in half so it fit in my stupidly small women's pants pocket. "Hello?" I answered without looking at the caller ID.

"You good?" Silver asked, the sound of the bar muted in the background. He must have called me from his office phone.

"Yep. How about you?"

"A few broken tables, but the hunters are paying for it."

"Thanks for checking in," I said, feeling my little heart warm from the gesture.

"Stay safe, girl," he ordered and hung up.

I checked my messages and quickly let Theo know what I was up to. She replied she was too stressed and just needed her bottle of wine and bath and would meet up tomorrow.

"Everything okay?" Grant asked.

I nodded and put my phone away. "Yes. Just checking in with friends."

"Your friend seemed not to like those hunters," Jong-min commented.

"Does anyone like hunters?" I asked. "They make most people nervous."

"True," Reed agreed.

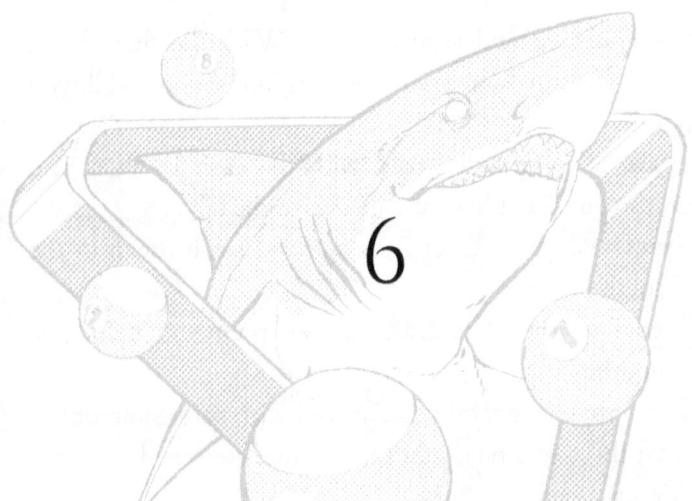

6

We finally made it to the restaurant, and I waved at Gina who stood behind the counter. She returned my wave, looked at the foursome following me, and whistled, while giving me a double thumbs up.

I groaned and shook my head. Gina was at least two hundred years old, a sea witch with very little power, who had survived thanks to friends with lots of power. She was still gorgeous, and I knew she was going to deliver the pizzas personally.

One of the booths was available and I pointed to it. "Why don't you guys snag that booth while I get the pizzas ordered? What kind of drinks do you want?"

"Beer pitcher works for us," Jong-min said.

I nodded and altered my course to go to the counter.

Gina leaned across the counter, her cleavage pushing against the v-neck shirt. "Where did you find those scrumptious boys?"

"Silver's," I answered honestly. "Back off, before I find out if I can get laid or not."

She chuckled and straightened. "Work the field, babe. I'm your backup, not your competition. So, what'll you have?"

I gave her our order, paid with the cash I'd won, and carried the pitcher of beer and glasses to the table.

Grant took the pitcher from me and set it down in the middle of the table.

Reed took the glasses and passed them out before he began pouring.

They worked so methodically and with zero communication, that there was no doubt they were a crew, or like, super best friends.

"Are you guys lovers?" I asked curiously.

"No," all four replied simultaneously.

"Best friends?" I asked.

They all nodded.

I raised my glass and smiled. "Cheers."

We all clinked glasses and then took drinks. Reed downed his entire glass and poured himself a new one.

"So, what's there to do for fun around here?" Grant asked.

"Well, besides Silver's, there's a theater, a fighting ring, and a few other bars," I answered.

"What do you do for work? Or are you just pulling scams?" Jong-min asked.

"Hey, it's not my fault men fall prey to women so easily. I do have a job, but that's classified," I said with a smug smirk.

Jong-min laughed and I loved the lyrical sound of his laugh. "You're very interesting, Ms. Kassidy."

"Kass," I corrected, and leaned my elbows on the table, giving him a perfect view of my cleavage.

His smile widened. "Kass."

"So, how come you wanted to get away from the hunters?" I asked and leaned back, beer in hand.

"They creep me out," Jong-hyun answered. "Bad aura and bad vibes all around from them."

"They're jerks, too. Think their crap don't stink," Reed grumbled.

"True, true," I agreed.

"What about you? Why were you so keen to get away?" Grant asked.

I swirled my beer and said, "I don't like them, and they don't like me. We always end up fighting, and Silver's bar paid the price last time."

"You're a shifter, right?" Jong-min asked and flared his nostrils. "Your smell isn't like any I've scented before."

"You don't visit the ocean often, do you?" I asked.

"No, we usually stay inland," Jong-min answered.

"I honestly thought you'd figured out what I was by my teeth," I said, and smiled wide so they could see them again.

"Lots of creatures have sharp teeth," Grant said with a shrug.

"Ah, well maybe I'll leave you in suspense? It'll continue my air of mystery," I said with a wink.

"Here are your pizzas," Gina said as she used her tentacles to carry all four pizzas, napkins, and plates to the table.

"They smell great," Grant commented, and started passing out the plates.

"Thanks, Gina," I said.

She let her tentacles slide back beneath her dress. "You boys better be nice to my girl here. She's got tough skin, but a good heart."

"Beat it," I said and threw a napkin at her.

She caught it and waved it as she walked away.

"Meddling pain in my ass," I grumbled, and pulled a slice of combination onto my plate.

"This is incredibly cheesy," Reed commented as he pulled a slice from the pie and the cheese stretched the entire way without breaking.

I added parmesan cheese to mine, nodded, and said, "Like I said, her pizza is the best." I took a big bite and moaned softly. "So good."

"It really is," Jong-hyun whispered as he ate his vegetarian pizza.

Jong-min nodded his agreement, his mouth full, so he couldn't verbalize it.

The silence was nice as we drank our beers and ate our pizza.

It was rudely interrupted when four massive guys sauntered into the restaurant. They talked twice as loud as necessary, or polite, and acted like they owned the place.

The pod. I hated them and they hated me. They were orca shifters, and only visited this area one week a year. I'd totally forgotten it was that time of year already.

"Crap," I whispered, turning away from the doorway and facing the back wall, and Reed, who was sitting there.

"What's wrong?" he asked.

"Loner Girl? What are you doing with people? Did you pay them to eat with you?" the leader of their pod, Nat, asked.

Technically, I had paid for them to eat with me. So, I stayed silent and continued eating my food.

"Oy, bottom feeder! I'm talking to you," Nat snapped.

Reed started to puff up, but I gave a slight shake of my head before turning and glaring at Nat and his pod. "Look, what I do with my money is none of your business. Why don't you go slink off and attack some defenseless penguins or something?"

"That's funny, coming from something that bites whatever it can, even if it's a human," he sneered.

"I don't eat humans," I said, and shook my head. "I actually have good taste, unlike you, who I saw following around Tracy last time you were here. Did you get medicine for your blowhole?"

He took a step forward and Reed and Jong-min immediately stood up.

"You're ruining our meal. Beat it," Reed snarled.

"Oh, acting tough to try to get with Loner Girl? Don't worry, man, she'll put out, even if you aren't tough. She'll take whatever physical contact she can get," Nat said while smiling salaciously at me.

I jumped over the table, grabbed Nat by the side of his neck, and yanked him down until his face smashed into the floor. Orcas were great hunters in the water, but he was clumsy on land, even clumsier than me.

"Fuck you," I snarled. "Just leave me alone."

His pod stepped forward, but so did Reed and Jong-min.

"You want to take this to the water and see who the winner is?" Nat asked as he straightened and dusted his clothes off.

I stood and shook my head. "No, I want you to leave me alone. I'd be ecstatic if I never saw your ugly dorsal again."

"Leave now," Gina ordered them. "I told you last time you were here, stay the hell out of my restaurant."

"Fine. We're leaving. I lost my appetite anyway," Nat sneered before leaving the restaurant.

"Sorry, Gina," I muttered, and looked down at my hands.

She patted the top of my head. "I'm surprised you didn't bite his hand off. No fighting in my restaurant ever again, though, got it?"

I nodded. "Yes, ma'am."

"Good. Everyone back to eating. Show's over," Gina announced as she headed back towards the counter.

I turned towards Reed and Jong-min, while also facing Jong-hyung and Grant and said, "I'm sorry for causing you trouble. Please excuse me."

With a quick spin on my heel, I walked out of the restaurant and back towards Silver's. I needed a drink ... or seven.

The orcas weren't allowed in Silver's, because they caused a lot of damage the last time they came through, so I knew it would be safe there.

"Back already?" Tonka asked.

"Don't want to talk about it," I muttered, as I sauntered past the line and right inside.

Several women voiced their displeasure, but there was nothing they could do about it.

The bar had filled up even more since I had left, and it required me to veer around people.

I finally made it to the bar top, and I slammed a fifty-dollar bill on the top in front of Silver. "Bottle."

Silver arched a brow. "What happened?"

"Orcas," I snapped.

He took the bill, turned and grabbed a bottle of my favorite liquor from the wall, and set it down in front of me. Since the bar was packed, he couldn't just let me walk around with a bottle, so I waited, impatiently, as he grabbed a large glass, added ice, and set it down. "No fights."

"Those college boys get escorted out?" I asked.

"The hunters were after them," Silver answered. "You won't be seeing them anytime soon."

I opened the bottle, poured until the glass was full, and screwed the cap back on. "Cheers."

Silver scowled, but a customer at the other end of the bar drew his attention.

Carrying the bottle and glass, I made my way to the far side of the bar, where a booth for two was always reserved for me.

I considered texting Theo, but if I did, she would leave her bath and wine behind to come drink with me, and I didn't want to ruin her night more than it already had been.

No, tonight I would drink alone and people watch.

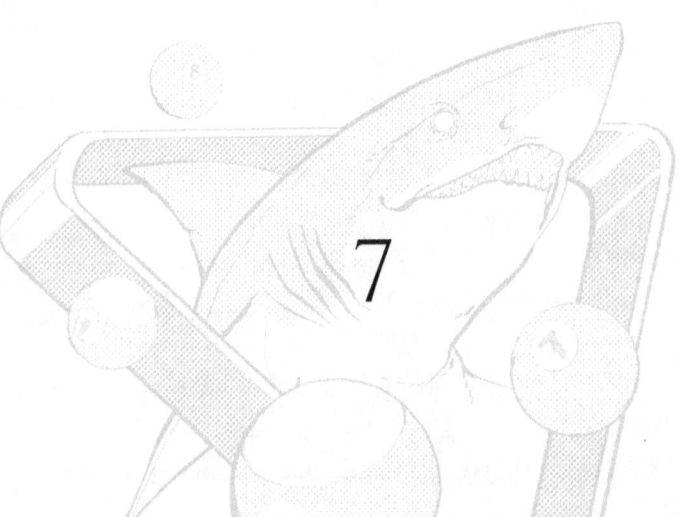

7

Children swarmed around the floor-to-ceiling tank to get a better view of the fish and me. I loved the children. They were so excited, happy, and legitimately carefree. Just how I tried to live my life.

Being careful not to act too out of character, I did a few flips in the water, earning adorable little gasps and cheers. They tugged on their teacher or parent's sleeves to get them to look, but I quickly resumed my normal swimming pattern before the adults looked.

The aquarium had installed live video cameras on most of the exhibits, but mine was one they kept private. It wasn't a good look if humans saw me climbing in and out of the tank each day. The nosey jerks would start pushing to advocate for shifters' rights, even though I didn't want or need their help.

As soon as the last visitor left the aquarium, Stacy, the manager, waved at me. She was a tall, thin woman who always wore a business suit, despite working at an aquarium. Her platinum blonde hair was neatly braided down her spine and not a single hair was out of place. Her teal eyes sparkled with magic, but I'd never been able to pinpoint what her magic was. Since she had given me a job and kept my secret, I didn't question what hers was.

Swimming to the surface, I shifted forms and shook my wet hair. "Hey, Stacy."

She held a towel in her hands, waiting for me to climb out. "Good evening, Kass. You made a lot of kids happy today. Thank you."

I smiled. "I'm glad. They're so cute that I can't help it, sometimes."

"Well, since they can't thank you, I'm doing it on their behalf."

"How's the aquarium doing, anyway?" I asked. At one point, they were about to close down, but business seemed to have picked up.

"It's doing a lot better. We even got approval to put a new exhibit in," she exclaimed, her eyes sparkling.

"What kind?" I asked nervously as I took the offered towel. My change of clothes were a few feet away, so as soon as I was dry, I'd change into those.

"Jellyfish," she replied, her eyes sparkling with excitement. "There are several different kinds, and I know it'll bring in lots of visitors."

"Or at least make them stay longer," I said and wrang out my hair on the tile floor with a drain nearby.

"Your payment was direct deposited," she said, before turning and walking away with a wave.

"Thank you," I called after her.

Once dressed, I walked out the back exit and hummed as I walked down the street.

Two blocks from Theo's apartment, I heard a woman scream and people started running past me.

"Vampires!" a man yelled as he ran by.

"Shit!" With adrenaline pumping through me, I raced the last two blocks, burst into the entryway of the apartment building, and took the steps three at a time. Finally, I reached the third floor, flinging open the door into the hallway, where I was met with the sight of three vampires' backs.

"I don't have any," Theo said calmly.

"You are a witch. You always have potions," an unfamiliar male voice said.

"I don't keep catatonic potions," she hissed.

The sound of flesh smacking flesh had me running forward, knocking the middle vampire to the ground and sliding into the middle of their circle.

Theo smiled at me from where she was, pinned to her front door with a vampire male's hand around her throat. "Baby, there you are. How was work?"

Okay, so we were trying to play this cool, got it?

"Work was good. Who are your friends?" I asked, sauntering over like this was completely normal.

"Oh, they were just leaving," Theo said. A powerful magical explosion burst out of Theo, knocking the vampire who was choking her across the hall and knocking the other vampires down. It didn't touch me, thanks to the spell she had put on the ring I wore.

I put my arm around her waist, cuddling up close like we were lovers so I could whisper in her ear. "I need to kill them?"

She shook her head and kissed my cheek. "I told you, Dom, that I don't keep potions here. If you want a potion, go three blocks west to the Witch's Hut, and they'll sell you some."

The vampires stood and dusted themselves off.

"Fine," he said. "Next time, keep some on hand for when I visit."

She scoffed and rolled her eyes. "I don't care whose dick you came out of. I'm not giving anyone special treatment. Go to the damn store like everyone else, or find some blood bag to do it for you."

He scowled, obviously not used to being treated in such a manner, but finally headed down the hallway and to the elevators.

"Inside," she said with a hissed breath.

I pushed the door open with my foot, spun us around while supporting most of her weight, and led her back into the apartment.

She waved her hand and the door closed while her ward also activated, preventing anyone from entering.

"What happened?" I asked as I gently lowered her to the couch.

She winced and adjusted her seated position. "They knocked, and I thought it was you. I was stupid and didn't check first, just lowered the ward and opened the door. He's one of the Original's sons and thinks he should get whatever he wants as soon as he wants it. Had my wards been up, he wouldn't have surprised me, and wouldn't have touched me."

"I'm sorry," I whispered. "What do you need?"

She waved her hand. "Just give me a minute to rest, and tell me what happened after I left?"

I sighed and plopped down on the couch beside her.

After telling her everything that had happened, she put

her arm around me and pulled me against her side for a hug. "I'm sorry. There are plenty of guys out there. Tonight, we can go to Silver's and you can scam a dozen people. I'll even put on my short skirt with the thigh-high stockings and fishnet shirt to get all the easy idiots' attention if you want."

I chuckled and hugged her middle. "You're the best."

"There was something about that foursome, though. I can't really say what it was, a feeling or something? It was a bit strange."

"Yeah," I agreed.

"How was work, really?" she asked.

"Good," I said, smiling softly. "I made a group of kids really happy."

"Water acrobatics?" she guessed.

I nodded. "This one girl in the front had cute pink bows in her hair. When I did my first spin, her mouth dropped open and she squealed so loud, I could feel the vibration in the water. Then, when they fed me, she had her pudgy little face smooshed right against the glass to watch as I ate."

"Sounds like you had a great day," Theo commented, and gave me one more squeeze before standing. "I'm glad."

"Yeah, it was a good day. The aquarium is getting a jelly-fish exhibit soon, too. That should bring in lots of visitors."

"Oh, I love jellyfish," she exclaimed, as she headed to her room to change.

"Where do you want to eat?" I asked. "Feeling like anything particular?"

"Mexican!" she said, and poked her head out of the room to look at me. "I really want some enchiladas."

"Enchiladas do sound yummy," I agreed. "I'm definitely ordering a margarita and some guacamole."

She fake gagged and ducked back into her room. "Guac is so gross."

"You'll still eat half my chips, though," I replied.

"We'll order separate orders of chips and salsa and chips and guac," she decided.

"Sounds like a great plan to me," I agreed, stood, and headed to the sliding glass door that led to the tiniest patio ever created. There was barely enough room for me to stand on it, let alone anyone else.

I looked out at the city and watched the people walking about. Humans, vampires, mammal shifters, aquatic shifters, witches, orcs, trolls, ogres, goblins, and so many more inhabited this world. This city had some of each, and for the most part, we all got along.

I still remembered when I'd slid onto the beaches here ten years ago. I'd gotten attacked by some great whites on a power trip, and had swum a few days straight to get out of their waters. I was small for a tiger shark, so other sharks tried to attack me often. Laying on the beach in my human form, I'd stared up at the starry night and wished I had friends. Wished I'd been some other kind of creature that had a herd or pod, or some community to be with.

Theo had found me naked and crying on that beach and taken me back to her house. She'd seen some part of herself in me, and our friendship had been immediate. If she hadn't shown me compassion and realized that what I needed was love and friendship, I'm not sure what would have become of me.

The orcas were right that I was normally a loner and craved physical touch almost more than anything else in life.

It was a curse, and I tried to keep those desires at bay as much as possible.

I was fairly certain that was why Theo touched me so much when we were together. She knew I needed it, and touch was one of her love languages, too.

"Ready?" she asked behind me.

8

I closed and locked the sliding glass door and smiled at my best friend. "Yes." My brain finally registered what she was wearing. Blue jeans, a bright pink halter top, and a long, white, curly wig. I arched a brow. "You're wearing pants?"

Once Theo had come out as transgender, she had fully embraced her femininity that she had so long repressed, and very, very rarely wore pants. She said that the pants made her feel restrained, and she would never let society restrain her brilliance ever again.

She put her hands on her hips, narrowed her eyes, and asked, "Are you trying to say I don't look fabulous?"

"Bitch, you're always fabulous, naked or dressed. It's just ... this is only like the third time in ten years I've seen you wear pants."

She ran her hands down her hips and looked down, her nervousness betrayed by the movement. "It's easier to carry talismans in pants, especially pants made for men, since the pockets are so big."

"Which is such bullshit," I grumbled. "Girls need pockets, too." The vampires must have upset her more than I realized. If I saw that blood sucker again, I'd tear his fangs out. For now, I needed to change the subject and get us back to our fun girls' night. "That wig is new, isn't it? I haven't seen you wear an all-white one before. It makes you look ethereal."

She flipped some of the curls over her shoulder and smiled. "Doesn't it? I got it on sale for half off, too! Can you believe that? Total steal."

I made my way to the door and nodded. "You should make the company pay you for wearing it because you know you're going to get a ton of people questioning where you got it. You should earn a commission."

After removing the ward, she opened the door for me and we walked arm-in-arm to the elevators. "I've been considering doing some modeling," she admitted.

"You totally should!" I exclaimed.

"Work has been so busy, I don't know if I would be able to make time for it," she huffed. "There've been three times as many customers this month."

"It is vacation time," I reminded her.

She shook her head. "No, this is something different. It's locals."

"Are they buying the same potions? Are there any similarities?" I asked.

"Lots of potions for defense and health, and talismans, too."

The elevator doors opened and we hurried outside; both of our stomachs rumbled and drove us to move faster to the restaurant, once finally outside of the apartments.

The cool night air blew our hair around, which made

Theo huff in annoyance. Knowing her, she'd likely spent hours styling the wig.

I pulled open the door for her and we were immediately seated by Charles, the host who was almost always working when we came.

"Fancied some delicious food tonight?" he asked.

"You know it," Theo replied as she sat.

He hadn't even bothered bringing menus, which was smart, since we had the menu memorized. "The usual?" he asked.

"Yes, but instead of just chips and guacamole, we'd also like an order of chips and salsa," Theo said.

He glanced at me with a knowing smile. "Tired of her stealing all your chips?"

I chuckled as Theo scowled. "I don't steal them *all*."

"I'll get your orders in with an urgency on your drink order," he said and spun away.

"I wish every place gave us such great service," Theo said, as she leaned her elbows on the table and set her chin in her hands.

"I want to go on a trip," I said, looking around at all of the people chatting and eating.

"To where?" Theo asked.

"I'm not sure. I just need to get out of town for a short time, I think," I answered.

The door opened as more patrons came in, but I didn't bother looking in that direction.

"I think you should stay in town for a bit longer, at least," Grant said as he pulled a chair up to our table and sat on the side to my left.

My eyes widened. "Grant? What are you doing here?" I looked around, but didn't see the other three guys.

"Well, I was hungry, but the others weren't, so I left them in the rental to find some delicious food. And it seems I lucked out, because I am going to get delicious food *and* be flanked by gorgeous women," he said, smiling wide and winking at Theo.

Charles set our drinks down and did a double take at Grant. "I didn't know you were having another guest. Can I get your order?"

"Just give me whatever Kass is having," Grant said, leaning back against his chair and crossing an ankle over his knee. He had on a pair of jeans and a t-shirt that told me Mr. Average was above average when it came to muscles. I could count his abs from here.

"So, how long are you and your friends in town for?" Theo asked.

Charles set our chips, salsa, and guacamole down. He returned a moment later with another margarita for Grant.

I dipped my chip in the guacamole, getting as big of a scoop as I could, and opened my mouth wide enough to fit it. My mouth could open much larger than a human's, so it wasn't hard.

"We aren't sure," Grant answered as he scooped out some guacamole on a chip for himself. "We're trying to find a new place to live, honestly."

Theo's eyes brightened. She loved gossip. "Oh? Did you get chased out of your last town? Wreck too many innocent girls' hearts? Deflower the mayor's precious daughter?"

Grant laughed and shook his head. "No, nothing like

that. It was boring there, and there weren't many options for us for work or dating."

"That does sound boring," Theo responded.

"Well, there's definitely a lot more prospects here," I said.

His eyes seemed to glow as he looked at me. "I have noticed that."

"You're a shifter, right?" Theo asked, saving me from my awkwardness. I was not good at taking compliments.

He crunched on another chip while nodding.

"What kind?" I asked.

He swallowed, leaned forward, and asked, "Are you asking me to strip for you, Kass? You should at least buy me dinner first."

I mimicked his movement and said, "I bought you dinner last night."

He leaned back and laughed loudly, gaining the attention of the other patrons. "True. True."

"So?" Theo prompted.

"Sorry, ladies, but this restaurant is not the appropriate place for that. However, if you allow me to enjoy your company for dinner, I will gladly show you afterwards," he answered.

"Well, in that case, I guess I'll allow you to stay," Theo said, and sighed dramatically.

"Wonderful," he said.

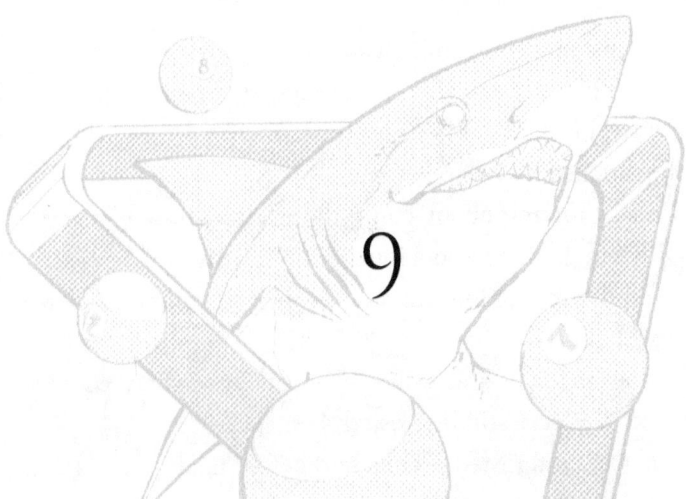

9

"So, tell me about yourself," Theo said. "What type of work are you looking for?"

"I spent a lot of time as a bodyguard," he answered. "Let's just say I can take a bullet or two to the chest without taking damage."

"Oh, kinky," she replied with a smile, and draped one arm behind her chair, relaxing, which was not normal when we were around a stranger.

"I've also been a janitor and a myriad of other things. I'm not too picky," he said with a shrug.

"I think I heard the aquarium is looking for a janitor," Theo said.

I cut her a glare, but changed it to a smile when Grant looked at me.

"I'll have to check them out sometime then," he said. "I've heard the aquariums are often relatively easy to clean for janitors because they don't have to clean the tanks since they have marine biology students cleaning the tanks."

"I will kill you," I whispered to Theo.

That just made her smile wider.

"You could also ask Silver," she suggested next.

Gently, I kicked her beneath the table.

She flinched and glared at me.

"I was thinking about going there after dinner," Grant said with a nod, his eyes looking off into the distance.

"Well, we're heading there after this, so you can accompany us," I offered.

He met my eyes and smiled. "Great! I can show you my other form if you're still interested then, too."

"Oh, she's interested," Theo said before taking a big drink of her margarita.

Grant laughed and I rolled my eyes.

"Excuse my bestie, she's been trying to get me out into the dating world for a while now," I said with a soft sigh.

"Not a fan of the dating scene?" he guessed.

I shrugged. "It's always harder for predators, especially ones like me."

"Oh? What type of predator are you?" he asked, genuine curiosity making him lean his upper body forward.

I smiled and said, "Sir, you've yet to even ask me on a date! I can't possibly bare myself in such a manner to a random man."

He laughed softly. "Of course not. My apologies."

Theo chatted with him about random things, mostly about her job as a potion witch, while we munched on our appetizers. By the time the food came, we were two drinks and two appetizer refills in.

It didn't matter, since we were all still hungry. I devoured every last piece of food, not even leaving a single grain of rice on the plate.

"So good," I moaned, and patted my full belly.

"It really was. I'm going to have to bring the guys here," Grant said.

Theo and I tried to convince him to let us split the check, but he demanded to pay the full bill, since he'd gotten to enjoy our company.

We couldn't say no to that!

Bellies full, bill paid, we waved to Charles and headed out of the restaurant to go to Silver's.

"So, about that strip show?" I asked with a smirk.

Grant looked around, headed into the next alley, and waited until we were out of sight before shifting into a hybrid form, part animal and part human. To our utter shock, his animal form was a white dragon.

"D-dragon?" Theo stuttered, her eyes glowing in the dark.

"Wow. I've never met a dragon before," I commented. "Your scales are gorgeous."

He had left his head mostly human, but when he smiled, he had his dragon's teeth, and I wondered if he did it because that was how my form was most of the time. "Yes, we are becoming increasingly rare."

"That happens when you decide to hide from humanity to protect and hoard your gold. Sort of hard to reproduce when you aren't allowing females to get within five hundred feet of you," Theo commented.

He shifted back and nodded. "Completely true. Another reason I refuse to stay in one place that doesn't have enough prospects for me."

"Thanks for showing us," I said.

"I'd show you my full form, but I don't have any spare clothes," he said as we headed back out of the alley.

"I mean, I wouldn't complain if you had to walk around shirtless," I said with a shrug.

He laughed and kissed my cheek. "Thank you."

I blinked up at him. "For what?"

"For not being afraid of me," he said. "Last time I showed someone my form, they ran away."

"What a moron," I scoffed. "You're stunning."

He beamed. "Well, I think of the two of us, you are definitely the most stunning."

"Yeah, she is really gorgeous," Theo agreed.

"Are you two an item?" he asked.

Theo shook her head. "Nope, just best friends."

He nodded. "Got it."

"Speaking of best friends, are you going to call your posse out?" she asked.

"Not sure," he admitted softly. "Sometimes they prefer to stay in. I'll let them know where I'm at once we get there, but then I'll leave it up to them if they come or not." He smiled at me and said, "Though, I'm not keen on giving up some alone time with you, so maybe I won't tell them who I'm with."

"Oh, you are smooth, dragon," Theo crooned. "I think I can already approve of you being with my bestie."

Grant stopped at the end of the line waiting to get into Silver's and I laughed, grabbed his arm, and pulled him past the waiting patrons.

"We don't wait in line," I whispered to him.

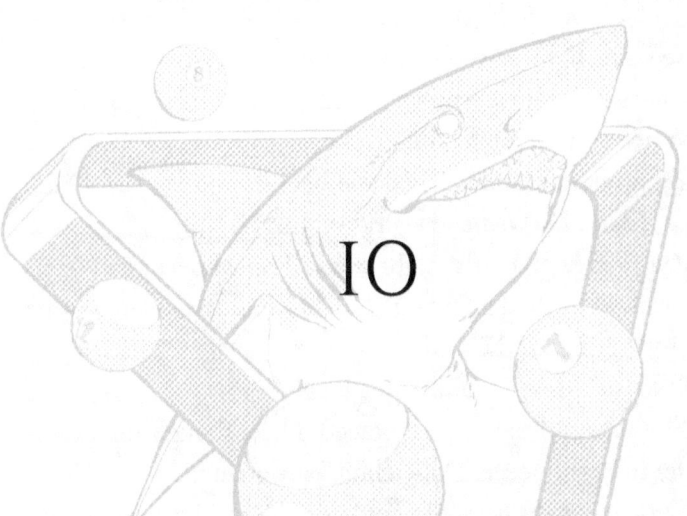

IO

Instead of Tonka, a terrifying and beautiful troll woman manned the entrance. The sides of her head were shaved, and the rest of her thick and glorious hair was styled into a mohawk, with some braided on each side to keep it more easily contained. She had thin tusks, a common trait among the females, and hers reached the bottom of her nose, a sign of her warrior heritage. The only jewelry she wore were two golden hoops, dangling from each of her pointed ears. She wore armor everywhere she went, even had a bikini that transformed into full battle armor with the touch of a button. Because Silver forbade her from carrying weapons, her sword sheath was empty, but she'd still put it on.

"Hey, Zyra," I greeted. I stepped forward as I released Grant, and hugged her.

She squeezed me tightly, my bones creaking. "Fishling!" she greeted. "It has been too long!"

"Is your twin here?" I asked, peeking over her shoulder and into the bar. Zyra had a twin sister named Zara who was her polar opposite. Instead of dressing as a warrior, she dressed in light dresses and refused to carry weapons anywhere. Of course, she was a powerful magic user, so she didn't need a weapon to kill anyone.

Zyra nodded and pushed me back to look at me. "Your eyes are dark. Do we need a girls' night?"

Zyra's idea of a girls' night was killing whoever had upset one of us. We'd had a few girls' nights, and they were always very refreshing for the soul.

"Not this time," I said with a laugh.

She released me and embraced Theo, though noticeably gentler in her squeeze. "Magicling," she greeted.

Zyra and Zara were the only ones allowed to call us such names. They'd earned it with their fierce loyalty to us, and the few times they had saved our asses.

She finally noticed Grant and arched a brow. "You brought a male?" She leaned forward and asked, "Is this part of one of your scams?"

My head fell back as I laughed and shook my head. "No, he's just a friend."

"For now," Grant said and held his hand out.

Zyra sized him up, then shook his hand.

I could tell from the way the skin color on his hand changed that she was gripping it hard, but his smile didn't waver and hers grew.

Apparently, he'd passed her strength check.

"Please, enter my father's business and enjoy yourselves," she said, released him, and stepped back so we could enter. Silver wasn't her biological father, but had found the twins abandoned on the docks when they were little and adopted them.

A girl down the line complained about us getting let in

and Zyra released a growl that had even the hairs on my nape standing on end. The girl immediately shut up and cowered behind the guy she was with.

With Grant trailing us, we headed to the bar, where Silver and Zara were.

Zara squealed when she saw us, set the glasses she'd been filling down, and ran around to hug us. "My beautiful friends!" she greeted and kissed our cheeks. "I've missed you."

"We've missed you, too," I said. My eyes widened when I realized she'd changed her hairstyle, adopting one similar to her sister's. "Your hair is different."

She glanced at her father before bending and whispering to us, "Trouble brews, friends. Keep your wits about you."

Well, that was terrifying to know that even Zara was preparing for battle.

"Who is brewing the trouble?" Theo asked, leaning her head on Zara's shoulder with a smile, so no one would think we were discussing anything other than friendly things.

"Girls!" Silver snapped.

"Busted," Zara squeaked and zipped back around the bar top to resume serving people.

Theo and I snickered as we approached Silver.

"What do you like to drink?" I asked Grant, turning so I could see him. I leaned my elbows against the bar and crossed my legs at the ankles.

He shrugged. "Just order me something that tastes good."

"Water it is," Theo teased.

Silver finished helping the customer next to us and then settled his gaze on me. "You good?"

I spun around to face him and smiled wide. "Right as rain during a hurricane."

"You are a hurricane," he muttered and looked over my head at Grant. "What would you like to drink?"

My mouth dropped. "Rude."

"I know what you want, girl," he said with a smile.

"I'll have whatever you make for these two lovely ladies," Grant said, and stepped up closer behind me, his heat pressing into my back.

"Three sparkly drinks coming right up," Silver said, and spun around.

I wanted to press back into Grant, but it was definitely too soon for that. No matter how long it had been since a man had held me.

"I'll go snag a table," Grant said.

"Okay," I agreed.

Theo and I watched him walk away, admiring his *assets*, and were both surprised when he went into the pool area.

"Oh, he meant that type of table," I said.

Theo laughed. "He probably wants to test you out. Maybe I should make myself scarce. There are quite a few hotties here tonight."

"That's up to you. I've got no issue with you staying with us. You know that."

She bumped her shoulder into mine. "I know, but I also know it's been a lot longer for you than it has for me."

My mouth dropped and she doubled over in laughter.

"Drinks," Silver said, drawing my attention away from Theo.

I grabbed my drink and Grant's, gave Silver a wink, and headed to the pool room.

"Go get 'im, girl!" Theo called after me.

Since both of my hands were full, I couldn't flip her off, so I turned and stuck my tongue out at her before spinning back around.

"Show him what you can do with your tongue, not me," she called out.

A few people whistled and I shook my head.

Grant had secured a table and was finishing racking the balls when I finally made it to him. He smiled when he saw me, and it lit up the entire room.

"I'm surprised you managed to snag a table," I said as I handed over his drink.

"You'd be surprised what some hovering and random growling will get you," he said with a smirk.

Wet panties.

"I'll have to remember that," I said. "Though, I don't have as much of a growl as you."

"No?" he asked. "What do you have that's frightening?"

I smiled wide. "Jaws of steel."

He laughed and held out a cue stick. "Sounds frightening enough."

"You want me to break?" I asked with a raised eyebrow.

"Oh, right. I forgot that you're a shark," he replied.

My heart froze and I blinked at him with wide eyes. "Huh?"

He chuckled. "Don't act innocent. I saw you hustle those college guys last night. You're a total pool shark."

"Oh, right! Yes. I am a pool shark on occasion. Well, why don't we place a bet on this game then? Make it more interesting." I leaned my hip against the end of the pool table and smiled up at him.

He crowded my space, leaned his hip against the pool table, and said, "I like that idea. How about winner pays for our date tomorrow night?"

"Date?" I asked, and folded my arms across my chest. "Pretty presumptuous of you."

He leaned closer and said, "Not presumptuous. Confident."

"What are we going to do on this date?" I asked, leaning a tad closer, so we were separated by a deep breath.

"Whatever the winner decides," he replied, his voice dropping lower and vibrating through my body.

I smiled, stepped back, and said, "Oh, I am going to take you on the wildest date you've ever been on, Scales."

"Promises, promises," he whispered in my ear, before stepping back and sitting on one of the stools against the back wall.

I bent over, exaggerating my bend so my butt was on full display, lined up my shot, and hit the cue ball.

Three solid-colored balls zinged into different pockets and the others spread out around the table.

I smiled happily at Grant, but he was giving me the same smile.

Oh, yeah. I was going to enjoy my time with him for sure.

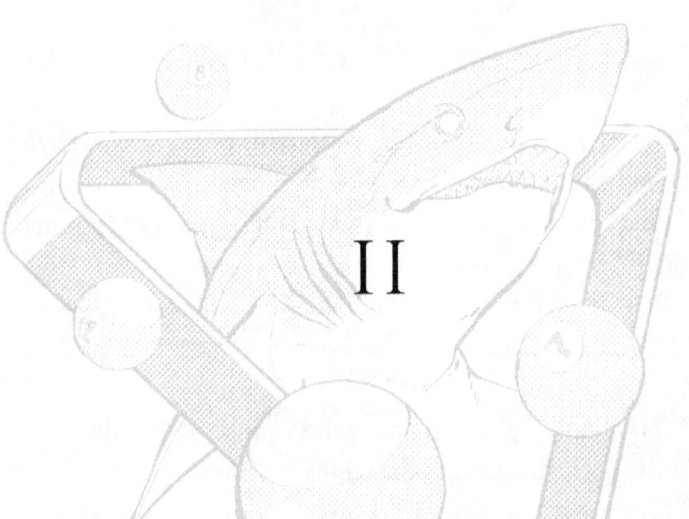

II

"You really are good," Grant said for the third time as I continued to stare in disbelief at the pool table.

Theo walked over to me and scowled. "What happened?"

I looked up at her, my eyes wide. "I ... lost."

She gasped and her hand went up to cover her heart. "What?"

I pointed to the one solid-colored ball, the green one, and said, "That's mine. I was even solids."

"He cheated. He must have," she said adamantly, her eyes narrowed as she looked at the table like she could replay what had happened.

Grant snickered. "Been a while since you've lost?"

I narrowed my eyes at him. "I've never lost before! How? How did you beat me?"

He smiled like the cat who caught the canary. "So, I'm your first?"

All of my disbelief disappeared and I burst into laughter, laughing so hard that tears streamed down my face.

"Can I get your number?" he asked and held out his phone.

"You should be throwing your panties at him," Theo mumbled and took a seat on one of the stools.

"That's tomorrow," I said, as I finished putting my contact info in his phone.

Theo laughed and shook her head.

"How about a second game? New bet?" he asked, smiling wide.

"You're on!" I shouted and started pulling the balls back out of the pockets and onto the table.

"This town is really nice," Grant commented as we re-racked the balls.

"It would be a lot nicer if the trash got taken out more often," a husky female voice commented.

Theo and I tensed, our fighting instincts kicking in immediately as we recognized the voice.

A ball still in my hand, I raised my eyes and glared at the rainbow-haired woman who stood at the end of our table. Koia was Theo's nemesis, a rainbow mermaid with immense magical power, and a hatred of Theo for no reason other than hating that Theo was more powerful than her.

"Piss off, Cod!" I snapped.

She cocked her left hip to the side, flipped her long and luminous rainbow hair over her shoulder, and asked, "Do you want some real company, handsome? I can't imagine this reject would offer you much. Unless you're into pity sex?"

"Fuck off," Theo snapped, standing from the stool and coming to my side.

"Language, ladies," she said. Darkness surrounded her as

she lifted her hand, pointed at Theo, and said, "Oh, right. You're not a lady. You're a transgender freak!"

Theo had been called names constantly once she came out, but no one ever called her names around me, because I wouldn't let it stand.

My fury consumed me and I jumped over the table, my body shifting to cover my arms, throat, and stomach in my shark skin. Fins grew out of my forearms, my dorsal fin grew out of my back, cutting a hole in my shirt to make room, and my face shifted into partial shark form. I clamped my jaw down on Koia's forearm, the one she still had raised, and shook my head once.

Her bones were like butter to my teeth and I spit out the part of her forearm I'd just bitten off, the part landing next to her hand that had been severed in the process.

Koia screamed, power swirled around her, and she tried to hit me with a shrinking spell.

Grant stepped between us, taking the spell instead, and he instantly shrank to only one foot tall.

Theo leaped forward, splashed a sleeping potion on Koia's face, and kicked her body away from us. She grabbed my shoulders and stared into my eyes. "Kass?"

Her blood tasted better than the sweetest sugary drink I'd ever consumed. It was full of power and my teeth ached to gnaw on her bones.

"Sweet," I said, and licked the blood that coated my teeth. "So sweet."

"Zara! Zyra!" Theo yelled.

The people around us had backed up until they were trying to disappear into the wall. Smart move on their part.

There were so many magical creatures in this bar who

likely had blood and meat just as sweet. So many juicy treats within reach.

"What's wrong with her?" Grant's tiny, now high-pitched voice asked.

"Mermaids like Koia have high magic and it makes them tasty," Theo whispered.

"Oh, bloodlust," Grant said.

Zyra and Zara stood before me, they looked at each other, the mess on the ground, tiny Grant, and back at me.

"Let us go on a walk," Zara said sweetly.

"Yes, we should walk under the moonlight," Zyra agreed with a nod.

"No one will care if I eat the rest of her," I whispered. "She's too tasty to waste."

"You cannot eat the customers," Zara said sternly. "Daddy told you that last year, remember?"

"Let's go outside and find another meal," Grant suggested.

I picked him up and tilted my head as I looked at him. For some reason, I didn't have the urge to taste him, even though I knew he had magic, too. "Why did you jump between us? I could have beaten her even at your size."

"I wasn't sure what type of spell she was using," he said and shrugged.

"You smell good, but not in the food way," I commented and pressed his body against my nose to inhale deeply.

He swatted my nose, but it didn't hurt. "Hey! Let's go outside and talk more about our date or something."

"Let me carry him," Theo said and held out her hand. Her pulse was loud in my ears and I saw her swallow hard.

I pulled him closer to me, farther from her, against my chest, and bared my teeth. "No! Find your own!"

"Outside," Zyra said. She glared menacingly down at me while holding a pool cue like a staff.

Cold air blew against me, drawing my attention to my right, where I found that Zara had opened the back door.

My belly was still relatively full from dinner, and while the mermaid would taste good, I didn't want to be banned from coming to Silver's.

I looked down at the unconscious mermaid, her blood slowly spreading from her arm, and sighed. "Fine, I won't eat her, but only because I don't want Silver mad at me."

Zyra nodded. "Good."

"Want to get some snacks, go to my hotel room, and watch movies?" Grant asked me.

"Your friends might get mad at me if they see you like this," I mumbled. "I don't want them mad."

He set his hand on my upper chest, the highest point he could reach, and smiled. "They won't be mad at you. They'll laugh at me. Come on, let's watch crappy movies and snack on super sugary foods."

With Grant clutched between both of my hands, I held him against my chest, and walked out of the bar.

"I'm not hungry," I told Zara. "You can go back inside."

"Mr. Grant, my father would like to speak to you tomorrow," she whispered.

"Okay," his high-pitched answer came out like a little kid agreeing to get a treat.

"Good night," Zara said, and kissed my cheek.

"The spell can be reversed, but I need to go to the store first," Theo said softly beside me.

"I'll have her text the address once we arrive, so you can meet us," Grant said.

Theo nodded, kissed my cheek, and ran down the alleyway.

"She was scared of me," I whispered.

"Yes," Grant agreed. "Considering you just bit someone's arm off and then considered eating every other magical being in the bar, I can understand."

"I said that out loud?" I gasped. "That was supposed to be internal monologue."

"You definitely said that out loud," he said with a chuckle. "Turn left down the alley."

Silently, I followed his directions and the farther we got from the bar, the clearer my head became.

When we finally arrived at the hotel he was staying at, I was completely back to my normal self and felt bad.

I stood outside the door to the hotel room he shared with Reed without knocking.

"I promise he won't be mad at you. If he is, I'll protect you," Grant said and patted my upper chest.

"I don't need your protection," I said and finally raised my heavy hand to knock.

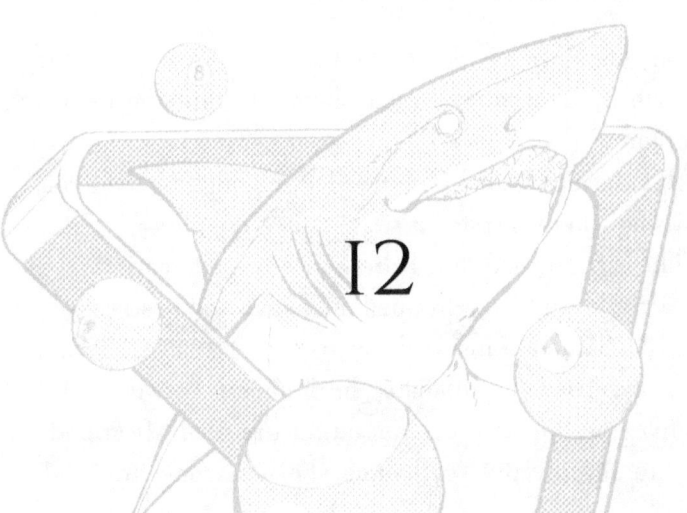

12

Reed pulled out his phone and quickly snapped a bunch of pictures, before bursting into laughter. He doubled over, clutching his stomach as he continued to laugh and tears rolled down his cheeks.

"Yeah, yeah. Laugh it up," Grant said and folded his arms across his chest.

The door between their room and the ones the twins were in opened and both walked in.

"What's so funny?" Jong-min asked. He stopped when he saw me and noticed Grant at the same time. "What did you do?" he asked. His eyes glowed bright red and I suddenly felt like I couldn't breathe.

I raised my hands in surrender, mouth closed, and breath held as I waited for him to relent. My legs started to wobble from the adrenaline pumping through me, so I squatted down, hands still raised with palms facing him. I could hold my breath for a long time, so I wasn't in danger right now, which was the only reason I wasn't freaking out. Fighting him would just make me look guilty, but I also wouldn't let him kill me. They had no idea I could hold my breath for a long time, which allowed me to fool them into thinking I was at their mercy.

"It's not her fault," Grant yelled, his high-pitched voice surprisingly loud despite his size. "Stop it right now!"

The air returned and I drew in a big, dramatic breath. "I'm sorry," I said, and dropped my hands and head simultaneously. "Someone insulted my friend. I attacked her and when she tried to retaliate, he jumped between us. I couldn't stop him or push him out of the way. My friend is going to reverse the spell once she gets some items she needs."

"You need to text her the address," Grant reminded me, still glaring at Jong-min.

I pulled out my phone, opened my text chat with Theo, and held it out to Reed. "Can you text it for me, please?"

He took the phone, his pointer finger slidding along my hand as he did so. "Sure."

I sat on the couch and rubbed my face. "This night went to shit so fast."

Grant grunted and when I looked up, he had little dragon wings coming out of his back and he used them to fly onto my lap. "It wasn't a complete waste," he said as he sat cross-legged and let his wings disappear.

"Does it hurt when your wings come out?" I asked.

"No," he replied immediately. "They just appear. Does it hurt when you shift your face like you did earlier?"

I shook my head side to side.

"Shifted face? What?" Reed asked.

"I made my mouth larger so I could bite her arm off," I answered. "My, um, other form has a large mouth."

"Still keeping that a secret, huh?" Grant asked and smiled up at me.

"Got to give you something to be curious about," I teased. Though, he should have figured out what I was when my fins came out.

"Why did you leave the restaurant yesterday?" Jong-min asked from where he still stood in front of the door. Even though Grant had vouched for me, he still looked like he was considering whether to attack me or not.

"I didn't want to cause you any additional trouble and those idiots had upset me," I admitted.

"You know we didn't eat with you only because you were paying, right?" Reed asked.

"I had hoped that wasn't the only reason," I replied with a slight smile that was only a little forced.

After a few moments of awkward silence, the doorbell rang and Reed hurried to let Theo in.

She smiled at all of the guys before hurrying over to me. "You okay?"

I nodded and smiled. "I'm good. Sorry for scaring you."

"You sure you can reverse the spell?" Jong-min asked with narrowed eyes.

"Yes," she replied confidently. "I'd suggest we move him off of Kass's lap first, though."

"Oh, fine," Grant said with a heavy sigh and stood.

I carried him to an open spot in the living room, set him down, and backed up.

Theo took out a small bag that smelled like several types of herbs, stuck the contents in her mouth, chewed, and then held her hand out towards Grant.

Purple light leached from her hand to Grant, and once it

covered him fully, his body instantly returned to its normal size.

Theo dropped her hand and spit the herbs back into the bag, tied it shut, and tossed it in the nearby trash. "There we go. All back to normal."

Grant pulled his pants' waistband forward, nodded once, and let go. "Thanks," he said with a smile.

"Well, it was sort of our fault for you ending up like that, so it was the least I could do," she replied with a shrug.

"You want to stay and hang out, too?" Grant asked.

She shook her head. "I've had enough adventure tonight. I'm going to go home, put my pajamas on, and chill."

"Sorry," I said.

"Don't apologize for sticking up for me," she snapped. "I was a second away from disintegrating her. So, you really saved me from getting banned from Silver's."

"Well, that's a good thing, then," I replied, and smiled wide.

She kissed my cheek and waved as she headed to the door. "Be nice to my girl, or that shrinking spell will be used on a single point on your bodies."

With that threat, she walked out and let the door close behind her.

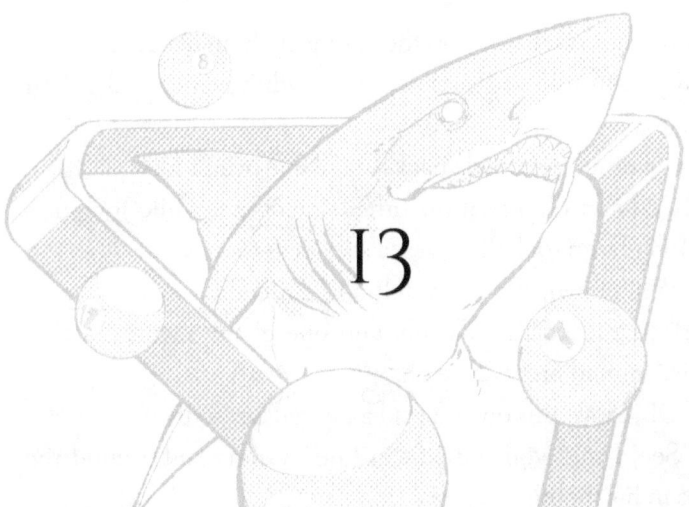

13

"Movie time!" Grant said, clapping his hands and rubbing them together with a gleeful smile.

"Snacks?" I asked.

Reed pointed towards the little kitchenette. "Have whatever you want."

The kitchenette counters were covered in snacks of all kinds, as well as drinks.

"Hello, snack bar," I said and hurried to pick some out. There was so much to choose from that I couldn't decide quickly.

Jong-hyun handed me a paper plate, and said, "I usually like to take a little bit of multiple things."

"I could hug you right now," I said as I started putting several types of chips on the plate.

"You could," he whispered so softly I almost missed it.

Instead of responding, I continued adding more snacks, moving down to the jerky section of the countertop next.

Once my plate was full, I grabbed a soda can, and walked

to sit on the couch. I sat on the center cushion because people usually preferred the outside, and I didn't want to take their spot.

The others grabbed snacks and came over, too.

Reed and Grant sat on either side of me, while Jong-min and Jong-hyun took the loveseat beside us.

"What movie are we watching?" I asked.

Reed turned the TV on, and one of my favorite action movies immediately came on.

"Oh, I love this one!" I said a tad too excitedly.

"See, I told you she'd fit in fine," Grant said around the chips in his mouth.

"What did you do tonight before the fight?" Reed asked.

Grant smiled wide. "I beat her at pool."

"You cheated somehow. You must have," I grumbled.

"What did you bet?" Jong-min asked while examining a chip on his plate.

"A date," Grant replied giddily.

"I demand a rematch," I said, and crunched my chip extra hard.

"We can have as many rematches as you want," Grant said and leaned closer to me. "I'll just keep increasing the bets."

"I won't lose next time."

"I want to play her next," Jong-hyun said.

Jong-min scowled. "I play her before you."

Jong-hyun nodded. "Right."

My brows furrowed. Why was Jong-hyun acting submissive to Jong-min? Was it a dominance thing? And did Jong-min really want to play against me, when his expression said he was still ready to attack me?

"I'll play all four of you." I shrugged. "I need some spending cash anyway."

"Shush, the movie is starting," Reed said.

Grant draped his arm behind my back, leaned close, and whispered, "He can recite this movie from memory."

"Me, too," I whispered back, turning my face so it was even closer to his, our mouths barely separated.

Reed leaned towards me. "Are those gills?" His finger brushed the side of my neck, just above my gills.

I shivered and nodded as I looked at him. "Yes."

"So, you're an aquatic shifter?" he asked.

"Shush, the movie is on." I winked at him, and tore off a bite of jerky.

Sitting in the hotel room with these four guys, I realized how comfortable I was with them. They were definitely the first guys I'd felt any sort of comradery with in a long time.

This day had been such an intense and emotionally draining one that my eyes started to grow heavy halfway through the second movie.

"What day is it?" I asked.

"Friday," Grant answered, and gently pushed some hair back from my face, his soft fingertips stroking along my cheekbone in the process.

"I have work in the morning," I answered and stood. "Sunday is my only day off."

"You can sleep on the couch, if you don't want to head all the way to your place," Reed offered.

I'd thought he was asleep until he spoke. "Sorry, I can't risk being late to work." I kissed Grant's cheek. "Text me the information for our date tomorrow."

He stood. "What time do you get off work?"

"Six o'clock," I answered, and headed to the door.

The twins were asleep on the love seat, leaned against each other, both with their mouths open. Taking a picture of them in such a position would probably upset them, so I kept my phone in my pocket.

"Want me to walk you to your place?" Grant asked.

"No," I snapped. Immediately, I took a deep breath to calm myself, since my reaction was likely not what he expected. "Thank you, but no. I'll be fine."

He kissed my cheek and opened the door for me. "I'll text you tomorrow."

"Thanks for tonight. It was fun."

He smiled sleepily. "Yeah, it was. Thanks for coming."

I raised my hand to him in goodbye and walked down the hallway. Instead of taking the elevator, I took the stairs to try to wake my brain up a bit.

The walk to the aquarium felt like it was twice as far, and like it took twice as long for me to strip and put my clothes into the locker they kept for me. I slipped into the tank and shifted forms before drifting lazily, allowing my brain to shut off, while my body moved on its own to keep water and oxygen going into my gills, and slept.

Sharks like me didn't sleep like a human did, but I could let my human brain shut off while my shark one took over.

When my shark eyes saw Grant, Reed, Jong-hyun, and Jong-min looking into my tank the next day amongst others visiting, my human brain instantly woke.

For a split second, I lost my control and shifted into my human form. It was so quick that no one else noticed, but the foursome had been staring straight at me. Their eyes widened and they started talking to each other animatedly.

In order not to raise suspicion, I continued my normal swimming path and kept my focus off of them.

Hopefully, they would just think it was their eyes playing tricks on them.

"Mommy that's her!" a little girl yelled. "My favorite shark!"

Making an unplanned circle, I swam back towards the little girl I had seen just the day before on her school trip. Thankfully, she was on the opposite side of the tank as the guys who were still watching me.

"Isn't she beautiful, Mommy?" the little girl asked as she smiled at me, standing as close to the tank as she could without touching it. They were very intent on visitors not pressing their hands or faces to the glass.

If I were a bird, I would have preened at her compliment. Since I wasn't a bird, I made another unplanned circle, crossing the sea turtle's path, causing it to change its path and the wide-eyed fear it showed almost undid my control over my predator instinct.

"She is pretty," the little girl's mother said. "Come on, let's go to the next exhibit."

"Can I please watch her swim a little longer? Please?" the girl begged, not taking her eyes off me.

Since she was being so adamant, I made sure to swim always in her line of sight while mostly resuming my normal path.

"Just another minute," the mother agreed and pulled out her cell phone.

Glancing towards the side where the guys had been, I saw it was empty, so I swam back towards the little girl, her eyes fixed on me, and did a flip.

She squealed her eyes bright. "She did it again!" she exclaimed.

Having drawn enough attention to myself for the day, I let my human mind drift as I swam the rest of the day. In order to see the clock, I had to swim to the back of the tank, out of the view of most visitors. Generally, I waited until I saw the crowds shrinking, since that gave me a bit of a heads up that it was nearing closing time.

When I felt it was close to quitting time, I swam towards the back. Instantly, I averted course since the foursome were standing in the back talking to Stacy.

Oh, no. I hoped she didn't tell them my secret. I didn't think she would, but if they had some sort of power that forced her to tell the truth, she might.

After they all walked away, I hurried out of the tank, dried off, and got dressed.

"There you are," Stacy greeted.

I spun around and breathed a sigh of relief to see her alone. "Why were those guys back here?"

"They were hot, right? Sadly, they were here to try to get a job, so I can't even consider dating them."

"D-did you tell them about me?" I asked.

Her hands on her hips, she glared at me. "Of course not!"

"Thank you." I exhaled a relieved breath.

"You sure you can't work tomorrow?" she asked with puppy dog eyes. "I've got a school doing a tour."

"It's my one day off," I reminded her. "I've got plans tonight that I'm hoping will keep me out way past morning."

Chuckling, she turned, and raised a hand in goodbye. "I'll live vicariously through you, then. Have a good day off."

With tentative steps, I pushed open the back exit door. Looking right and left, I didn't see the foursome, so I walked out and pulled my cell from my pocket. Grant had texted, telling me to wear a swimsuit, and to meet him at the Cornerstone Beach in thirty minutes.

Thankfully, I could use my shifting ability to form scales over my breasts and lower body to create a makeshift bikini. Since I didn't have a house, I didn't have many clothes. I kept most of my important stuff at Theo's house since she said she didn't care. Owning a lot of things had never appealed to me, and since most of my life was spent in water, that prevented me from really owning much, anyway.

I messaged Theo to let her know I wouldn't be stopping by. She immediately messaged me back demanding I provide all the juicy details afterwards.

I flagged a taxi down for a ride to the beach, which was across town. After paying him, I headed across the parking lot to the public bathroom.

The last time I'd been down to this beach was over a month ago when Theo had begged me to go tanning with her.

I ducked into an open stall in the bathroom, stripped out of my clothes, and focused as I forced my shark skin to appear exactly where I wanted it to. It took a lot of focus, but once it was where I wanted, keeping only that part shifted was easy. Outfit fixed, I put my clothes into a paper bag the store clerk had been nice enough to give me for free.

The sun was beginning its descent, but the heat of the day still pressed upon me. While I preferred warm waters, there were times when hot weather was too much for me. Today was warmer than usual, but not unbearable.

I made it to the beach and was happy to see it relatively empty. In the water stood four familiar figures, all shirtless and wearing just swim trunks.

"Bless whoever created them," I whispered.

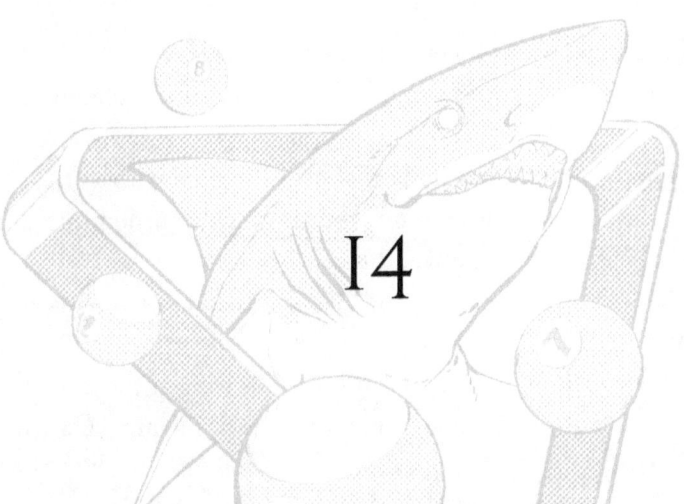

14

Even Grant was ripped. Who knew that those chiseled abs and arms lay beneath those clothes?

Reed noticed me first and waved.

I waved back and walked onto the hot sand. My feet instantly burned and I wished I'd left my sneakers on. Sadly, they were in the bag, so I just jogged to reach the guys – and the water – faster. "Hey," I greeted. The cool ocean water slid over the top of my feet, and I exhaled in relief.

"Hello," Grant greeted and kissed my cheek. "How was work?"

"Good," I said, trying to keep my smile normal.

"Anything interesting happen?" Reed asked.

I shook my head and walked deeper into the water. "Nope. My work is almost always boring. What did you guys do all day? Sleep?"

Jong-min scoffed. "We looked for work, actually."

My mouth dropped. "I'm surprised that information isn't classified."

Grant and Reed laughed.

I could get used to seeing all four of them shirtless.

"Are those ... part of you?" Grant asked, and pointed at my chest.

"Um, yes, my boobs are part of me," I replied with a grin.

He looked up with a scowl, but it quickly turned into a smile. "I meant your bikini ... thing."

"Yes, those are part of me. It's cheaper than buying a bikini."

"They look hard," Grant whispered, staring at the line of shark skin on my shoulders. He glanced up at me. "Can I touch it?"

"They are hard, and it's rather early in our date for you to ask for groping privileges," I teased and walked a little deeper into the surf. "So, what's the plan?" I asked, and kicked a little bit of water at Grant who flinched back.

"We are going to play volleyball," he announced with a proud smile.

"There's an odd number," I pointed out.

"We're going to take turns sitting out," he explained.

Two women in their early twenties hesitantly walked over to the twins. "Excuse us," the tallest one said. "Aren't you two—"

The twins nodded, not even letting them finish their question.

"Would you like a picture with us?" Jong-min asked.

"Are they celebrities?" I asked Grant softly.

"They used to be."

He didn't elaborate, so I saved that info to push the twins for later.

Grant, Reed, and I headed to the volleyball court while we waited for the twins to finish with their fans.

"So, who is on my team?" I asked. Somehow the volley-ball court sand was cooler than the rest of the beach. Knowing the city developers, they'd likely paid someone to enchant the sand there to increase visitors.

"Me," Grant replied. "It's my date, after all."

"I have to admit that I was surprised to see everyone here," I said.

"You'll find we do most things together," his voice dropped lower and there was absolutely zero doubt in my mind what he meant.

"Good to know," I replied huskily.

"Sorry," Jong-min said as they jogged over.

"No worries, rock star," I teased.

"Ready?" he asked, instead of responding to my teasing.

I dug my feet into the sand, spread hip-width apart, and made a super serious face. "Ready."

"No shenanigans. I'm the referee," Jong-hyun said sternly.

I raised my hand, shaking it back and forth.

He arched a brow. "Yes?"

After lowering my hand, I asked, "If we participate in shenanigans, what's the punishment? I'm not opposed to spankings, but I'd like to be able to sit, at least."

His mouth popped open for a brief second before he snapped it closed and softly whispered, "Just ... no shenanigans."

"So, no spankings?" I asked and stuck my lip out in a pout.

"Bets?" Reed asked. "I think we should make bets."

"You just want to spank her," Jong-min mumbled.

Reed smiled so wide I thought he might split his face.

"Wait, we have to confer," I said and walked closer to Grant, so we could whisper.

"What are you thinking?" he asked.

"Well, if it's something we both have to give, I'm not sure what to bet," I admitted.

"How about, loser buys the drinks tonight?" he suggested.

"Yes!" I agreed, almost shouting.

He chuckled. "Or dinner?"

"It's like you know the way to my heart already," I said and pressed a hand to the middle of my chest. "Should I be worried?"

He leaned closer and whispered, "Only if you don't like the thought of spending an evening with me."

"If I didn't like that idea, I wouldn't be here," I said, tapped my finger against his nose, and skipped away from him, so I was on one side of our half of the court.

"What's your bet?" Reed asked.

"You go first," Grant said and crossed his arms.

"If we win, we get individual dates with Kass," Reed said.

My mouth almost dropped open as I looked at Jong-min. "You're okay with that bet?"

He frowned. "Yes."

Arguing that he didn't seem interested and was still giving me the cold shoulder wouldn't be helpful, so I just closed my mouth.

"If we win, you buy dinner and drinks for me and Kass tonight," Grant said.

"Deal," the four of us said simultaneously.

"Let the games begin!" Jong-hyun shouted.

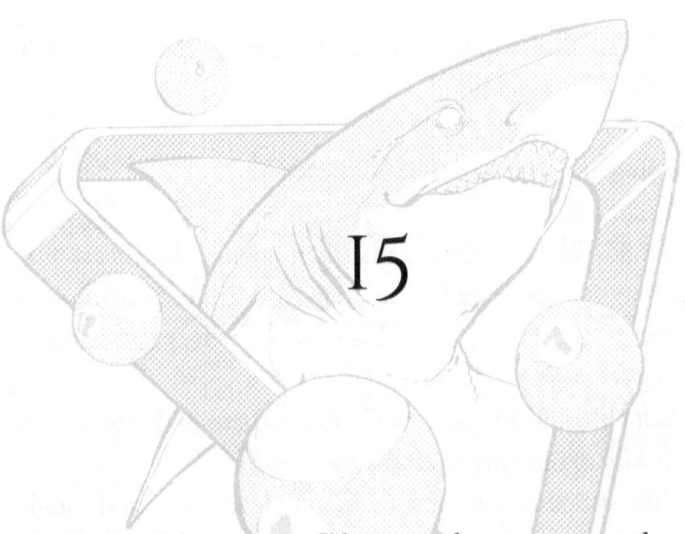

15

When he told us to start, I'd expected someone to grab one of the volleyballs from the sidelines. I did *not* expect the three playing to partially shift forms and Jong-hyun to create a magical barrier around the court.

"Uh," I said intelligently as I stared at them, surprised to say the very least.

Reed had shaggy gray fur covering his upper chest and neck, and his head was completely wolfen. He had left his stomach and arms human, which I was certain he'd done for my viewing pleasure, and I was completely okay with that.

Grant now had scales covering him from his stomach, all the way up to his neck. His feet were now clawed dragon's feet, and his head was a partial dragon's head with human lips and tongue. I hadn't known there were others who were capable of such intricate shifting. I wondered why he didn't let his wings out, but guessed it was probably because it would give him an unfair advantage in the air.

Jong-min was the most surprising as black feline ears had

popped out of the top of his head and a long, black feline tail now swished behind him.

"C-cat?" I gaped.

"You going to shift or not?" Grant asked.

I hesitated.

I could shift like they had. I had spent a lot of my life perfecting my control when it came to shifting. Shifting like they had would expose what I was, though. If they had seen me today, though, they already knew.

"I don't think I need to shift to compete with you all," I said cockily to hide my nervousness.

They stared at me for a moment, clearly seeing through my bullshit.

"You'll regret that after the first round, guaranteed," Jong-min said. A haughty smile spread across his face as he asked, "Unless you *want* to lose?"

"Let's go," I said. "I'll win in this form. *Guaranteed.*"

Jong-hyun tossed the ball up over the middle of the net and whistled. The ball was at least five feet above the net in the air.

I had never seen volleyball started this way, so I froze, uncertain what I should do.

Grant, Reed, and Jong-min all jumped up into the air, about three feet above the net, hands raised, as they all aimed to hit the ball.

My frozen state turned into one of extreme lust as I watched the three of them, their muscles flexed, and bodies stretched up over the net.

"I need a freaking camera," I whispered to myself, trying to burn the image into my eyes and memory.

Grant and Reed both hit the ball, pressing against it and each other as they began to descend back towards the ground.

An airwave from the force of their hits made me stumble back a step and my eyes widened.

This was not a typical volleyball match, even for shifters, which made them even more interesting and enticing.

Grant grunted and was able to angle the ball slightly to the side, causing it to veer away from our side and straight towards the other side of our opponents' court.

Jong-min dove with his arms outstretched, parallel to each other and touching from elbow to wrist. Somehow, the crazy cat-shifting superstar managed to get to the spot before the volleyball and sent it back up into the air.

Watching the arc of the ball, I realized it was headed towards the back of our side of the court. Grant had just landed, but wouldn't make it in time, so I dashed to the back, arms out to return the ball.

Despite running and diving, I barely made it before the ball came down. It slammed into my forearms and I grunted with the effort to send it back up into the air. My forearms felt like they were going to crack with the force, but I knew they weren't. My skin also burned with the spin of the ball and I regretted not shifting to my shark skin, which would have prevented the burning pain completely.

The ball sailed up into the air and Grant jumped up, in the perfect position to spike it over the net.

Reed jumped up with arms raised to block him, eyes narrowed and focused.

Grant suddenly adjusted his arms and hit it up for me to hit over instead.

With a wide smile, I jumped up, arm pulled back as I prepared to spike it with all of my power.

Jong-min jumped up, his arms raised as he put himself in the perfect position to block me.

"Not today, Satan," I whispered to myself, shifted my position slightly, and spiked the ball diagonally out of his reach and right on the line of the court.

"In!" Jong-hyun yelled, raised his arm, and pointed at our side. "Point."

Grant raised his hand and I took the invitation to jump up and smack his hand in a high-five.

"One point means nothing," Jong-min said with a deep scowl that had his brow furrowed and his ears half folded down.

"It means I beat you even in my unshifted form," I reminded him and strutted backward to get into position at the back half of the court.

"That is one nice ass," Grant muttered. "I could watch her walk away all day."

That was me, Kass with the nice ass.

I spun around and smiled brightly. "I told you I didn't need to shift to win."

"One point is hardly winning," Jong-min said, and rolled his eyes.

"What is winning?" I asked.

"First to five points," Grant answered.

"Do we do serves now or do you guys just always toss it up?" I asked, my head half-tilted.

"Serving just results in huge holes in the sand, someone getting a bone broken, or some other mishap," Reed responded before Grant could. "We do the toss-up to make it a little more fair."

"Alright, let's get that second point!" I shouted.

Grant winked at me, turned around, and crouched down.

Jong-hyun had run over and grabbed the ball while we were talking, so we stood, tensed and ready.

Jong-min's tail swished back and forth behind him, while his ears were high and alert.

Did he shrink to a normal cat size, or was he larger, like most werewolves I knew?

I grew in size when I was in my full shark form, so I knew it was possible. Going from a one-hundred-and-twenty-pound woman to a six-hundred-pound shark was sort of impractical when you thought about it. Magic was super insane and often made no sense.

Jong-hyun whistled and once again Reed and Grant jumped up to try to get control of the ball.

This time I was prepared for the maneuver, and dug my toes into the sand, as I shook my arms out.

Reed grunted, his forearms flexed and veins flared, and managed to hit it away from Grant and towards the left side of the court.

I ran over and dove with my arms out, but it hit the ground before I could.

"Point!" Jong-hyun called with his arm pointed towards their side.

Hopping up, I dusted the sand off and returned to my spot.

"We'll get it next time," Grant said confidently.

If I partially shifted, I would be stronger and could jump

farther, but my pride was too strong to give in when I'd told Jong-min I would win without shifting.

Jong-hyun looked to each side, confirming we were ready, and then tossed the ball up again with a shrill whistle.

After three more points went to the other side, I gave in and partially shifted.

Closing my eyes, I let my tail and dorsal fin come out, my face shifted a little more shark-like, and my teeth got bigger, too.

"You've got stripes," Jong-hyun said, and took a few steps towards me.

"Yes, I do," I agreed and gave him a small smile.

He stopped moving, cleared his throat, and returned back to his spot. "The score is four to one."

"You ready to flip this?" I asked Grant.

As I looked towards them, I realized it wasn't just Jong-hyun who'd been staring. All three of them were silently staring.

I clapped my hands together. "We playing, or do you guys forfeit?"

Jong-min shook his head, his eyes narrowed, and he said, "I never forfeit."

"Ready?" Jong-hyun asked.

"Ready," the three males said, though I could see them all casting glances in my direction every few seconds.

I would take advantage of their distractedness and score as many points as I could.

The ball went up into the air and this time, I used my tail to help propel me even higher up into the air. My jump put me up higher than Grant and Reed, who looked up at me with wide eyes. With focused determination, I slapped the volleyball right towards Jong-min with as much force as I could.

Let him return that!

"Fuck," Jong-hyun whispered from the sidelines.

Jong-min had his arms out, but at the last minute dodged to the side, out of the way of the ball.

The ball slammed into the sand, spinning its way deep down, until the hole was at least five feet deep. Smoke billowed up out of the hole and no one moved.

"P-point," Jong-hyun stuttered and raised an arm in our direction.

"Fucking dinosaur tits," Reed whispered as he stared at the hole.

"I am not a dinosaur," I said and crossed my arms over my chest.

"What was that?" Jong-min demanded and stalked towards the net.

"What?" I asked. "I hit it."

"You aimed for me!" he shouted.

"I aimed for the corner where you were," I agreed with a nod. "And?"

"You were trying to injure me," he growled and the hair on his head stood on end.

"A hit like that shouldn't have injured such a strong man as yourself," I said with a sweet smile.

His glare deepened, but he shut up.

Reed squatted down over the hole that had now stopped smoking. "How deep is that?"

Grant walked under the net to get a closer look. "Ten feet?"

"Is the bottom shiny?" Jong-hyun asked, as he also peered into the hole.

"It's glass," I explained. "Are you guys able to get it out or do you need my help?"

"She hit it so hard that it spun so fast and hot it turned the sand to glass," Grant whispered.

They all looked at me.

Unable to resist fidgeting, I squirmed and rubbed my thumbs over my stomach.

"You sure we can trust her?" Jong-min asked Grant.

Grant stared at me, silent, for several long and tense moments before saying, "I'm not sure."

"Um, you can't kill me on a date. That's like ... totally a serial killer thing to do. Plus, Theo will hunt you all down until she's obliterated every single one of you if you hurt me."

"No one is going to hurt you," Grant said and smiled.

"Could we, if we tried?" Reed asked.

"I was able to steal her air yesterday," Jong-min said.

I winked at him. "Sure you were."

His eyes narrowed again and his eyes started to glow.

With a roll of my eyes, I walked under the net, set my hands on either side of the hole, and used the water in the sand to push the ball up out of it. The ball shot up into the air with a puff of water behind it, which sprayed the four guys around me.

I caught the now deflated, partially melted ball with one hand and smiled broadly. "You guys got a spare?" I saw one off to the sidelines, so I grabbed it and said, "Alright, game is back on. Time to win this!"

"What the ... " Jong-hyun trailed off, his wide eyes focused on me.

I tossed him the ball and winked at him before walking back under the net and returning to my spot.

"I didn't think she could get hotter," Grant whispered.

"Right?" Reed muttered and walked back to his spot.

"Ready?" I asked, smiled wide, and showed off all my beautiful, white, serrated teeth.

16

The sun set fully and I finally scored the final fifth point to win the game.

Grant and I high-fived and I shook my ass ridiculously as I danced my victory dance.

"Yes, you won," Reed conceded.

Jong-min scowled and for a moment, I thought he looked ... disappointed.

"That match took longer than we expected," Grant admitted. "So, we'll go eat dinner now. Maybe next weekend you can play against Jong-hyun?"

"Sounds great!" I agreed. "I just need a restroom to change in before we go to eat."

Grant nodded. "We actually wanted to change, too. Are you comfortable changing at our hotel?"

"Sure," I agreed with a nod.

With Grant at my side, we headed down the busy streets towards their hotel building. Despite it being crowded, there was an odd dark cloud of fear over the town. Did it have to do with what Zyra and Zara were talking to us about?

Was the trouble they'd mentioned more progressed than we realized?

I would need to see if I could get them alone to find out what they knew. Silver didn't like spreading gossip, but I needed information.

"The game was fun once I got the hang of how you play," I admitted. "I hope you guys are really up for playing next weekend."

"Definitely," Jong-hyun said with a nod.

"Maybe we should change the team up, so Jong-min gets a chance at redemption," I suggested.

He glared at me, but did not respond.

"Are you in the mood for any specific food?" Grant asked me.

I shook my head. "I'll eat whatever. Everything sounds good right now."

"What about you guys?" Grant asked as he looked up restaurants on his phone.

"If you tell me what you want, I can recommend my favorites," I suggested.

"What's something we haven't had recently?" Jong-min asked. "I'd like to try something different tonight."

"What about curry?" I asked. "Have you guys had curry before?"

"It's been years since I've had curry," Jong-hyun whispered.

"I know just the spot!" I said.

It took an hour for everyone to get changed and ready to go. As I stood in the entryway surrounded by the foursome, I realized I was very underdressed.

"You should have told me to bring nicer clothes," I grumbled to Grant and fussed with my shirt.

"What you're wearing is perfect," he said and kissed my cheek. "You look hot in whatever you wear."

"Thank you," I whispered as he opened the door for me.

We made our way to the restaurant, and I waved to the elderly couple who owned the restaurant and ran it.

It was practically empty, so we had our pick of tables. There weren't any large tables, so I moved three small ones together to create a large one.

"You sure they won't mind?" Jong-hyun asked.

"I've known them for many years. They don't mind," I assured him, and sat.

As soon as we sat down, the wife, a kitsune with white ears, approached. "Evening, friends," she greeted us, her nine tails fanned out behind her.

"Evening," they all responded.

She looked at me and smiled wide. "Daughter."

"Mother," I greeted, and dipped my head respectfully.

"Your usual?" she asked.

"For me, yes. My friends have not eaten here before, though," I explained.

She looked at the twins, leaned close to me, and whispered, "I approve of these two."

"Mother!" I snapped.

She giggled like a school girl, turned, and over her shoulder said, "I'll bring a feast for my adopted daughter's friends."

"Adopted daughter?" Jong-min asked.

"My first night on this land, Theo brought me here. Mother

took one look at me and announced that I was now her daughter, and she's done a lot for me over the years. I refused to live with her for more than a few days, though, since they didn't make much at the restaurant at that time. In an attempt to repay them, I got more business for them. Now, their business is flourishing, and I visit them at least once a week and update her on my life."

"And she does not care that you are currently eating with four men at once?" Jong-min asked, his eyebrow raised.

"A woman must taste the many spices in life before settling on the ones she favors," Mother said as she returned with a kettle and several cups carried by each of her tails.

With a groan, I dropped my head to my arms.

She tsked. "Serve tea like a proper lady."

Jong-min scoffed. "She is not a proper lady."

Mother quickly dropped the kettle and cups towards me and I was barely fast enough to catch the cups all in a stack in one hand, and the kettle in the other. "I rescind my statement that I approve of you. You are rude, and need to remember the lessons your mother taught you. Would you disrespect a daughter to her mother in your homeland? No. So, do not disrespect mine to me. She may be from the sea while I am from the land, but my heart cares not for her origin. Her soul sparkles, and men such as yourself do not get to diminish her shine."

Oh, snap! I'd rarely seen her angry, and I was totally enjoying the cowed expression on Jong-min's face.

He bowed his head and spoke too softly to her for me to hear.

Jong-hyun bowed his head as well as he said something, too.

Why was he bowing? He hadn't even said anything.

Mother scoffed and turned to examine Reed and Grant. After a narrow-eyed examination, she turned to me and said, "It figures you would find a dragon. You need fire to combat the one that rages in your soul."

With that, she spun and returned to the kitchen.

Quickly, silently, and carefully, I set the tea cups down and served them tea.

I started to pour my own, but Jong-hyun took the pot from me and poured it instead.

"I apologize for insulting you," Jong-min said softly.

I asked, "What did she say to you when you were whispering?"

"That is private," he whispered, and turned his head to the side.

Was that a blush on his cheeks? Had she really railed into him, even in those whispered tones? I needed to learn how to do that.

"So, do you know your birth parents?" Reed asked.

I shrugged. "Only until I was about ten years old. I tried to find them after that, but sea creatures are often born in the sea in their animal forms, and stay most of the time in those animal forms, since the human side doesn't come out for a few years. By the time I was able to search, mine were too far gone to try to find them. I have vague memories now, glimpses, but those could be created by me, too, at this point."

"I never knew mine," Grant said. "Dragon eggs can take decades to hatch, and are left in caves with dozens of other eggs. We break out of our eggs, walk out of the cave, and adapt from there. We do have a vague image of our parents that's seared into our brains, but it's often so vague because we only saw them through the shell."

"You two are pretty similar in several aspects of your life," Reed said with a nod.

"We are?" I asked. I mean, obviously we were similar in not knowing our parents, but what else?

"Stop giving away my secrets," Grant hissed. "I've got to maintain my air of mystery."

A laugh escaped and I shook my head. These guys were something else.

We sipped our tea, and I was enjoying my time with the guys when the door opened and two hunters walked in.

Father was standing at the counter and immediately shouted at them in his native language. The hunters glared at him, spoke back in the same language, and continued to enter.

17

I stood and headed towards them, preparing to fight the hunters if they threatened my adopted parents.

"Sit!" Mother hissed.

I froze, but did not turn around.

"We just want to eat," one of the hunters said. He looked at me, the foursome at my table, and back at Mother. "We will not attack or hurt anyone who is currently in this establishment."

"If you do, we will remove your heads," Father barked, and stabbed his knife into the table. It stood upright, quivering back and forth. Father was a dragon shifter, but unlike Grant, his dragon had no wings. He could still fly, though, thanks to the magic that coursed through his veins.

"Your adopted parents are pretty awesome," Reed whispered.

I took my seat and sipped my tea. "Yes, they are."

"Why are so many people drawn to you?" Jong-hyun asked.

With no proper answer, I just shrugged.

"It is her beauty and fiercely loyal heart that draw others to her," Mother said as she brought out appetizers. "Plus, she has a nice shape, no?"

The guys looked at me and she started laughing.

"Is business well?" I asked her to distract from her question and their looks.

She nodded. "How is work? Still good?"

I nodded back.

"You know you can always come work here and live in the apartment upstairs for free," Father said as he brought out more food.

"Your offer is appreciated, but I enjoy my work," I said for the thousandth time.

"What do you do for work?" Reed asked and leaned forward.

"I'm a model," I said.

Father muttered something beneath his breath that had Mother smacking him on the arm before they walked away.

"A model?" Jong-hyun asked.

I nodded. "Of sorts. People pay to see me in my natural habitat." Taking a sip of my tea, I refused to say more even as their curious stares bore into me.

"So, what do you like to do for fun, aside from taking money from idiots who underestimate you at billiards?" Reed asked.

"I like watching movies," I answered. "I probably spend half of my free time watching new movies."

"What do you like to watch besides action movies?" Grant asked.

"I watch pretty much everything," I admitted. "Gory B-movies are my favorite."

"Mine, too," Jong-hyun replied with a wide smile. "Zombie ones are my favorite."

"They're so bad that they are amazing," I agreed with a vigorous nod.

"Exactly!" Jong-hyun yelled and immediately ducked his head when the hunters looked in our direction. He picked up a piece of vegetable tempura and crunched on it while staring at the table.

I wanted to tell him to be as loud as he wanted, but didn't want to embarrass him more than he already was, so I kept my mouth shut.

"So, what is on the agenda for the rest of the evening?" I asked instead, holding the hot tea cup in my hands.

"That's a surprise," Grant said and smiled devilishly.

"Alright, then, keep your secrets," I replied.

Father came out carrying a tray loaded with dishes. "Your food, would-be suitors."

I choked on my tea, and that made him laugh as he finished setting them down.

"Rude," I hissed.

He patted my head and spun on his heel to return to the kitchen for more.

"It smells wonderful," Jong-min commented and started scooping a bit of each of the foods onto his plate.

"I recommend trying a little of everything before serving yourself too much. That way, you can gorge on what you really like." Having eaten here so many times, I already knew what I liked, so I piled my plate high with my favorites.

Once my plate was full, I dug in with reckless abandon. Everything was better while it was hot, and I refused to waste my chance at delicious food consumption.

The guys commented to each other about which foods they liked and I enjoyed watching the friends interact.

Father brought out more food and we ate every single piece on the table.

I relaxed and sipped my tea, while the others finished what was on their plates. What was it about these four that made me feel so calm? It wasn't often that I felt safe around people, and to find four of them at once was unheard of.

It didn't have anything to do with their races, since they were different types. They were all shifters, so maybe it was a weird kinship I had with them because of that. That didn't really make sense, though, because I hated the damn orca shifters, and don't even get me started on dolphin shifters.

Grant walked up to the counter, and I was certain he was paying for our meal while also trying to get onto Mother's good side. He didn't need to bother, since she just wanted to find me any male at this point. According to her, I was wasting my good years and my good eggs.

"A word outside?" one of the hunters asked me.

I flinched, since I'd let Grant distract me and the damn hunter had surprised me.

"Me?" I asked and looked up into his dark eyes.

He nodded.

Reed started to stand, but I held up my hand to him and stood. "It's okay. The hunters aren't here for me. Right?"

The hunter dipped his head and turned to look at Reed. "I am not hunting this female. I will not cause her harm, so long as she does not attack me."

I patted Reed's arm. "I'll be right back."

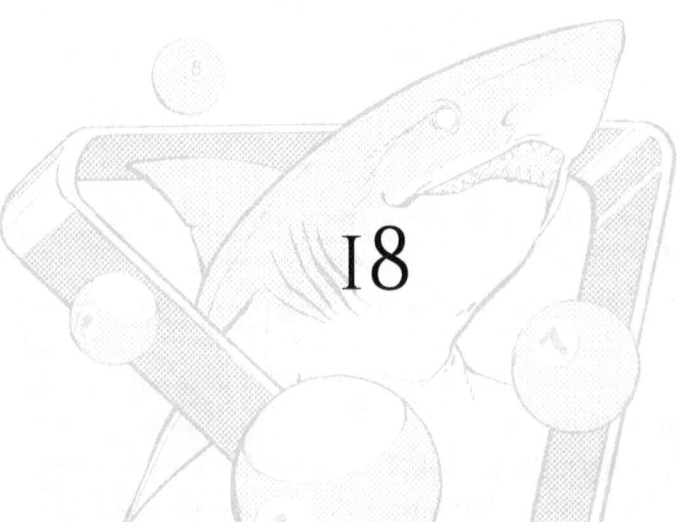

18

The hunter and I walked out of the restaurant, and once we were outside, he turned and scowled at me. "You are an aquatic shifter?"

I nodded. "I am."

"Have you heard of Bastian Zayne?"

A chill went up my spine at just the mention of his name and I bared my teeth. "It is not wise to speak that name within a mile of water." Gods, I wished I didn't know that damn name.

"There are rumors of his return. Have you heard anything or seen anything?" the hunter asked.

Now that we were outside, I was able to get a better look at the hunter. He was average height, well built, had a set of twin blades on his hips, and a hilt of silver sticking up out of his right boot. If I were to guess, I would say he was a dhampir.

"I have not heard or seen anything," I answered. "I pray that what you have heard are only rumors. His return would spell certain disaster to whatever region he sets foot in."

The last time I had seen him, I had barely swum away with my sanity intact.

"Let this be a warning, aquatic shifter. Word is he is headed this way."

"That's why you're here, in this town?" I asked.

He nodded. "There are more of us coming."

So, they weren't here to mess with Theo. That was good to know. However, just because they were here on a tip about Bastian didn't mean they weren't willing to spend the time fucking with her either.

"I'll keep my eyes open," I said softly.

He held out a white business card. "Our job is to protect the realms. Call upon us if you hear anything."

I nodded and tucked his card into my pocket. "I don't want him anywhere near my town, so I hope you catch him before I see him."

We both returned inside, and I was surprised to see the foursome waiting by the front register with Mother and Father all scowling at us.

I raised my arms and spun in a circle. "Not a hair out of place."

Father growled and returned to the kitchen.

Mother waved me over, and once I was on the opposite side of the counter from her, she whispered, "They hold pain and fear that I think you are to help them heal. Do not push too hard or waste this opportunity. Understand? You are losing out on your fertile years."

I groaned and let my face fall into my hands. "You could have stopped before that last sentence."

"I want grandchildren," she said with a huff, and then

started saying something in her native tongue I didn't understand.

"Thank you for the food," Jong-min said and bowed his head. "Your hospitality is much appreciated."

"Protect my child when she is with you," she ordered him. Her tails glowed, and then her entire body became covered in the light. "Or I shall rain pain unlike any you have experienced before."

She was incredibly scary when she wanted to be. Even I was shaking a little at her power display.

All four of the guys bowed their heads and said, "Yes, ma'am."

"Bye, Father!" I called, and waved to him.

He waved without looking at me.

Once outside, Grant asked, "What did that hunter want with you?"

"An old nemesis is supposedly headed this way," I answered, and started skipping away from the restaurant and towards their hotel. "He was asking if I had heard anything and to warn me."

"Did he know the person was a nemesis of yours?" Jong-min asked.

"He is a nemesis to all aquatic shifters," I whispered and stopped skipping. "He thinks we are unclean and wants to kill us all." He'd almost succeeded, too. With his power, he had almost boiled the seas dry. He had torn me apart, but I'd managed to escape while someone else sacrificed themselves for me. It was a sacrifice I would never ever forget. It was one I planned to repay someday ... in blood.

"I know who you're talking about," Reed said softly. "We

aren't going to say that name so close to the open waters, though."

I smiled and nodded. "Yes, let's refrain from that."

"Were you one of the …" Grant paused a moment before finishing. "… tortured ones?"

I nodded. "Yes."

Pain. So much pain and blood. Bits of my body spread out on the ground around me.

"That was over a decade ago," Jong-min whispered, snapping me back to reality.

"Slightly before I came here," I agreed with a nod, my voice shaky.

"You were a teenager then, right?" Reed asked.

"Yes. Yes, I was."

Jong-hyun growled softly and then asked, "Are you in need of a hug?"

I turned and looked at him curiously. "Huh?"

He opened his arms. "Hugging helps alleviate the pain of past memories sometimes. Your friend is not here, so I am offering myself as a temporary replacement."

I mean, it wasn't often a hot guy offered to hug me, and I *was* in need of a hug.

With a nod, I stepped into his open arms, and he wrapped them tightly around me.

"You are safe in this moment, Kass. They are not here. You are with friends," Jong-hyun whispered into my ear as he held me against his chest. His arms were like a warm barrier against the night and helped me push my memories away.

"Thank you," I said quietly as I stood in his embrace, my arms tucked up against my chest.

"We have all dealt with trauma in our past," he whispered into my ear. "It is not weakness to accept warmth from another to push away those painful memories."

When I attempted to step back, he let me go, smiling down at me. I stood on tiptoe and kissed his cheek. "You are a good friend," I said, and spun away, so none of them could see my face. With a deep breath, I shoved all of the emotions attempting to break free of their cage back down into that dark hole where they belonged. Normally, only Theo was able to break that seal, but tonight was a reminder that there were others who could cause the walls to crumble, and I needed to work on reinforcing them.

"Would you like to come back to the hotel and watch some movies?" Grant asked as he caught up to me.

"Sure," I agreed, turning to give him my best smile.

He draped an arm around my shoulders, pulled me close to his side, and whispered, "When you're with us, you don't have to worry about your safety. I hope you know that."

I looped my arm around his waist and said, "I'm more worried about you, Dragon. What if a pirate discovered you and tried to steal you from me? I'd have to fight to ensure he didn't take my prize from me."

"Are you saying you'd have to fight a pirate to protect your booty?" he asked with a smirk.

I looked around his shoulder, being extra dramatic with how much I leaned down at his butt, and said, "It is a nice booty. They wouldn't know how to handle it properly."

"I highly doubt we'll run into any—" Grant's comment was cut off as my favorite park came into view.

The park had two volleyball courts, a basketball court, and several weight lifting areas. It was mostly frequented by the shapeshifters who were focused on working out to get as muscular as they could.

At night, the area was owned by Cap'n Two-Teeth's Chums, a ragtag pirate crew of shark shifters with a gambling and alcohol problem. Cap'n Two-Teeth was an old great white shark with one eye, a hook stuck in his dorsal fin, and only two teeth left in his decayed gums. Normally, he should have grown the teeth back, since great whites often shed teeth, but he'd pissed off the wrong selkie who had been owed a favor by a sea witch, and now was cursed to only have two teeth at any one given point. The crew was loyal to him without question, and I loved them more than I wanted to admit. The only pirating they did now was finding ship-wrecks and making money off those finds.

"Oy! Who goes there?" a deep voice called out. Several dark, hulking shapes moved within the shadows, heading us off.

"I got this," I whispered to the foursome. "Don't attack them, please."

With a deep breath, I let out my dorsal fin and my tail, then strode forward and smiled wide, so they could all see my teeth. "It is I, Kass!"

19

"Kass!" several yelled, and the yell was passed down until it made it all the way through the crew that was spread out over the beach.

"Where she be?" Cap'n Two-Teeth hollered. He hobbled out of the darkness, his upper half fully shark, while his bottom half was mostly human. The hook in his dorsal fin was rusted now, and I wondered if it made him sick. He told me he would never remove it, but wouldn't explain why.

"You old dog! Have you brought my money?" I asked as I stepped forward, my accent growing to match theirs.

He narrowed his eye at me. "Your money? You owe me from our last night!"

"You've gone senile!" I shouted as we continued to walk closer to each other.

"Senile! I'm as quick-witted as the day I was born!" he snarled.

"I *would* liken your mind to a babe's," I teased.

Now that we were within arm's length, he spun around

and I did the same, our dorsal fins slapping together in our version of a high-five.

When we spun back around to face each other, the Chums erupted in cheers.

"'ave you come to drink with us?" he asked cheerily.

Drinking with them was always fun, but I wasn't certain how the foursome would handle them.

"No, sadly I've got other obligations," I said, and jerked my head towards the foursome, who were staring at us.

The Chums lit their lanterns, illuminating the entire crew of two dozen shark shifters for the foursome to see. Every single one of the Chums was partially shifted into their shark forms, and many bore scars from their many battles at sea.

"I see you're hunting your own booty tonight," Cap'n Two-Teeth teased.

Tilting my head back, I let out a bark of laughter. "Right you are, Cap'n."

"You sure you can't come have just one drink?" Trent, a hammerhead shark with a penchant to eat too much, asked.

"She still owes me an arm-wrestling match!" Shamus, an older great white who was the first mate of the pirates, shouted as he stepped into the lighted area.

"I beat you last time!" I shouted back, and crossed my arms over my chest.

"You did not!" His upper lip pulled back to show off his teeth.

"You sure have some interesting friends," Grant said from behind me. I glanced over my shoulder to find him and the other three about a foot behind me.

Cap'n Two-Teeth, Trent, and Shamus jumped. Had they not seen the foursome approach?

"You move mighty quietly," Shamus said, his shark head tilted, so he could look at them with one of his eyes.

"Stealth is always a great tool," Jong-min replied.

"You're after these land loving boys?" Trent asked. "You know you could have your pick of any of the Chums."

"Why do I feel like we were just looked down on?" Reed asked.

I chuckled. "Because you were."

"You don't look capable of handling a fiery, man-eater like Kass," Cap'n Two-Teeth said while looking down his nose at them.

"How about a challenge?" Grant suggested. "I win, and you accept I'm worthy of Kass and I continue on our date tonight. You win, and we'll leave her here to drink with you, instead."

"What?" I asked, my eyebrows zooming up into my hairline. Was he really making bets with the Chums right now about what my night entailed?

"What type of challenge?" Trent asked.

"You know you don't have to do this, right? We can just continue on our date without this?" I asked Grant as quietly as I could.

"You don't think I'm going to win, do you?" he asked and shook his head. "So little faith."

"I hardly know you," I reminded him. "Plus, I drink with them all the time."

"Then it won't be an issue if I lose," Grant said. "Which I won't."

This night just kept getting crazier and crazier.

"Come on, let him win your company for the night," Reed said.

"How about an arm-wrestling match to replace the one you wanted with Kass?" Grant suggested to Trent.

Trent laughed. "You'll regret that, land dweller. Kass, you might as well find a spot on the sand and get comfy for the rest of the night."

"If you're arm-wrestling, it's got to be against me," Shamus said. "Since I'm the reigning champion."

I rolled my eyes. "I'm the champion, and you know it!"

"Well, he ain't going to wrestle you," Shamus retorted.

I threw my hands up and walked back until I was between Reed and Jong-min.

"I accept," Grant said.

The Chums cheered, and we followed them onto the beach, where a few tables were set up. They usually played cards on them, but the cards were moved out of the way so Grant and Shamus could arm-wrestle.

They sat across from each other, and both wore wide smiles.

"You sure about this?" Shamus asked Grant. "You could have just walked away with your tail tucked between your legs and continued on your night with her."

"She's still trying to figure out if we're a good match. This should give me a few more points," Grant replied.

These guys were something else. Even though we hardly knew each other, they seemed to be trying to integrate into my world. It made me feel special, but also made part of me worry there was another ulterior motive.

"Ready?" Shamus asked and set his giant arm on top of the table, a fin sticking out the back of his forearm.

Grant set his arm atop it and grasped hands with Shamus. "Yes."

"Your pretty boy looks nervous," Cap'n Two-Teeth commented. "Maybe he should have offered to take up the challenge."

"Who are you talking about?" I asked, looking at the three guys around me. "They're all pretty."

The Chums laughed.

"You should leave a couple here for us," Freddy said, a salmon shark with a love of pretty guys.

"You'll have to take that up with them," I said. "I'm not their master."

"Definitely not," Jong-min scoffed.

"Oh, that one is feisty," Freddy said. "You can stay if you want."

"Let's begin!" Cap'n Two-Teeth said.

Everyone cheered, and I saw several making bets with each other.

"You better win this," I mumbled to Grant. "I still need dessert."

"Go!" Cap'n Two-Teeth yelled.

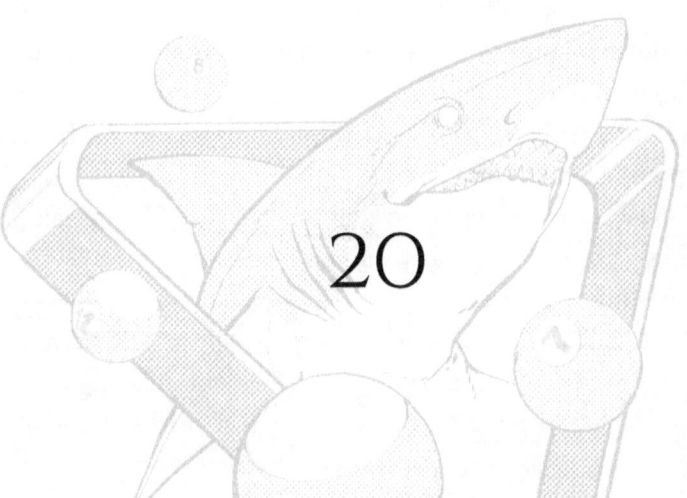

20

Grant and Shamus's arms flexed and everyone started cheering for who they wanted to win.

"You're not going to cheer him on?" Reed asked.

"You look a little pale," Shamus commented, his voice a bit strained.

"It's from my mom. She was always pale," Grant replied, voice even and body, except his arm, relaxed.

"Would you take this seriously?" I grumbled. "I'm in need of a drink or three."

"I'll give you whatever alcohol you want to drink after I win," Shamus said.

Grant chuckled. "Better hurry up, so she doesn't get even hangrier."

Was it hangry if it was drink based?

With a grunt, Grant slowly began pushing Shamus's arm, and then slammed the back of his hand into the table.

Several groaned, some cheered, and I just stared in disbelief.

Yes, I had beaten Shamus, but only because he'd been

worn down by others. I was strong, but not stronger than the old Great White.

Grant stood and several of the Chums patted his back and praised him for his victory.

"Well, looks like we get to continue our date," Grant said, as a huge, proud smile nearly split his face.

"My hero," I teased.

"Looks like they might be strong enough to protect you after all. I'll bid you safe travels and hope your pillaging goes well," Cap'n Two-Teeth said with a dip of his head and a wink.

"I'll be back next week," I said, and waved to the rest of the crew before motioning for the foursome to follow me.

Grant walked at my side, beaming like the cat who ate the canary.

Once through the park and back on our way, I turned to look at their expressions. "So, what did you think of the Chums?"

"Pirate shark shifters," Reed mumbled and shook his head.

I nodded. "Cap'n Two-Teeth's Chums."

"That's ... that's their name?" Jong-min asked.

I nodded again.

"They seem fond of you," Jong-hyun commented.

"As shark shifters, we try to stick together. There was a time that humans and mages almost hunted us to extinction. Witches kept killing us for our body parts for spells, too. Sharks aren't exactly pack animals, but we convinced our human sides it was necessary to survive. Those like Cap'n Two-Teeth did better than most by making a pirate crew. As a loner, they accepted me as an outsider, but they still don't trust me fully. I tried to fit in, but no matter how hard I tried, I'm a loner in the ocean."

And I had just shared way too much personal information with them. What was wrong with me? I wasn't even drunk!

"Yet you seem to have found a few pack members on land," Reed commented. "Pack isn't always the same race as you. Pack is often those that you find and share a bond with. Like us; we aren't similar shifter types, but we've banded together and formed our own pack."

Pack. That was something that sharks didn't have, but my human brain wanted one. Why? Why was it so hard for me to accept a solitary life?

"I should be able to accept a solitary life," I whispered.

"Yet, you're going on a date with four guys at once," Jong-min commented.

He hadn't said it maliciously, but it still hurt my feelings a little.

"I was asked on a date by one person," I countered. "You three were here when I arrived. So, it was your own decision to be here."

"I wasn't trying to insult you," Jong-min said.

I gave him my best smile and said, "Don't sweat it, kitty cat. I've got thick skin." While technically true, my feelings were not so thick-skinned. I wanted to be tough and not care what people thought of me, but I couldn't.

Theo was certain I had some type of mental health thing, and I refused to admit to her that I had gone to a psychiatrist and psychologist to find out. To discover my diagnosis of PTSD, Borderline Personality Disorder, and anxiety. It shouldn't have made me feel less, but I didn't want her to know what my issues truly were. Having a mental health issue that couldn't be fixed made my already problematic view of myself even worse. I'd done a lot of research once I had been diagnosed, and understood why I reacted the way I did a lot better thanks to it. That did not mean I could stop it, just that I understood where it came from.

Brains were so fun, right?

"What's your favorite drink?" Grant asked, changing the topic drastically.

"Whiskey lemonade," I answered immediately. "But Silver keeps making drinks I fall in love with more and more."

"Good to know," Grant replied.

Grant led us to a bar I'd never been to that was closer to the center of downtown. It was a really popular spot for locals and thus not a good spot for my pool shark tendencies.

The bouncer eyed me as I walked in.

"Don't get your tusks in a twist," I snapped. "I'll behave."

"You better," the troll growled at me.

Reed growled at him and the troll bouncer shut up and let us enter without further delay.

The building was at least twice the size of Silver's, with two bars on the lower floor, both with four bartenders serving patrons.

"Let's find a table," Grant said, placed his hand on my lower back, and steered me towards a set of stairs I hadn't noticed when we walked in.

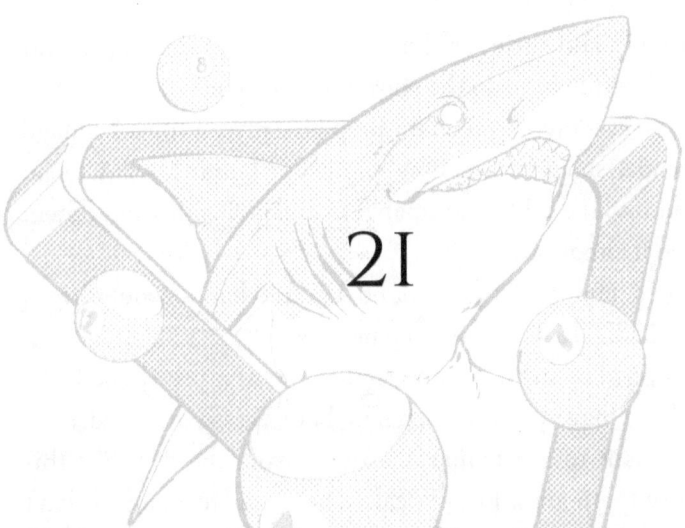

21

Up the stairs, we found a surprisingly quieter section with a bar, some chairs near the rail that overlooked the first floor, and a room in the back that had yet another bar, a u-shaped sitting area with coffee tables, and dark lighting.

"This is likely a vampire area," I whispered to Grant.

He pushed me towards the u-shaped sitting area and said, "They should have gotten here by now if they wanted this spot. Now, they'll have to fight us for it."

Vampires were one of the most terrifying races to me. They could suck your blood, steal your magic, and mesmerize you in minutes.

"Don't worry, vampires won't bother us, and if any do show up, you will be protected," Jong-min whispered in my ear as he walked by me and took a seat on the plush leather couch.

I huffed and said, "I don't need protection. I just don't like starting unnecessary fights." Okay, a total lie, but they didn't know me well enough to call me on it. Instead of scooting in and sitting by Jong-min, I forced Grant to sit and then sat beside him, on the edge of the u-shape.

It was a defense mechanism to give myself the advantage of escape, should an enemy show up. I didn't want to be tucked into the table and unable to escape if shit went down. Which it almost always did.

Reed and Jong-hyun found us and handed out drinks before taking seats across from me.

I sipped on my drink and smiled. "This is pretty good."

"Wait, have you not been here before?" Grant asked.

"This is my first time. I usually avoid the bars like this because there are a lot of locals who frequent it, and I don't want to start drama with people who live here. Visitors and those on vacation are a totally different story, though."

"Can't scam someone more than once if they frequent a spot," Jong-min mumbled.

"Exactly," I said and smiled wide.

"How did you learn to play pool so well?" Grant asked.

"When I first came here, Silver let me play whenever I wanted, even during times he was supposed to be closed. I slowly picked up things and taught myself how to play, and over the years improved my game more and more. There was a tournament held at the bar five years ago and one of the pro players offered to teach me. He was just trying to get laid, but I used him for his knowledge and then left him hanging. With my new knowledge, I started playing tournaments, but the money wasn't nearly as good as pool sharking."

"How much do you make doing that?" Reed asked.

"Depends on the weekend, and how many out-of-town visitors there are. Sometimes I can make a hundred dollars a night. Sometimes I can make a thousand a night."

All of their eyes widened as they looked at me.

"A thousand a night?" Grant asked.

I nodded. "Spring break is my favorite time of year. So many drunk, horny college students willing to throw money at women to try to get laid."

"That's ... brilliant," Jong-min whispered.

"Sometimes it is wonderful to be a female," I said with a smile.

"Do your teeth cause you issues?" Jong-hyun asked.

My smile dropped and my lips covered my teeth. I nodded and turned away, taking a long drink. "Yes."

"Can you shift them like you do the rest of your body?" Grant asked.

It was then that I realized between talking with the Chums and entering the bar I had shifted. My shifts often happened without conscious thought, but it bothered me when I didn't realize it.

"No," I admitted. "My teeth will not turn into human ones. This is the smallest I can make them. My only options are to make them bigger, and when I shift into more of my shark self, I have more of them, too. I've tried, but they won't turn blunt like a human's. Theo's tried to help me, but it just won't work."

They stared at me in thought and I wondered what they were thinking, but didn't want to ask. Some men were intimidated by my teeth. Some were scared I was going to bite their tongues if we kissed.

I was very careful with my teeth, and never bit anyone I didn't intend to.

"What is your favorite drink?" I asked Grant, since no one else had spoken.

"Martini," he answered immediately. "With at least two olives and *extra* dirty."

"Lie!" Reed sang.

Grant said, "Okay, my favorite drink is a strawberry daiquiri."

I chuckled. "Daiquiris are good."

"What is your favorite fruit?" Grant asked.

"Watermelon," I responded immediately. "What about you?"

"Peach," Jong-min and Jong-hyun replied simultaneously.

"Cherry," Grant answered.

"Pear," Reed said.

"Favorite season?" I asked. I normally didn't like playing twenty questions, but it was fun to hear their different answers.

"Spring," Jong-min and Jong-hyun answered simultaneously again.

Did they always answer like that? Were they really so similar, or did this have something to do with how Jong-min acted superior to Jong-hyun?

"Fall," Reed said after a moment of thought.

Grant tapped his finger on the table a few times before saying, "I guess summer, but not a super hot summer."

"What about you?" Jong-min asked me.

I had no hesitation in answering. "Winter. I love the rain, and when the sea is crashing and thrashing with high waves."

"Are you the type to sit inside and listen to the rain while covered in a blanket with a hot drink or the type to dance outside in the rain?" Grant asked.

"Maybe one day you'll find out," I said and downed the last of my drink.

"You're in our spot," a deep voice said beside us.

I looked up at the three guys and one girl who had stopped by our table, expecting to find vampires, but found dolphins instead. I *hated* dolphins.

Leaning back against the seat, trying to look as relaxed as possible, I said, "Weird, I didn't see your name on the table."

"I didn't know you could even read," the girl sneered.

"There are no reservations on tables," Jong-min said. "If you wanted this table, you should have gotten here earlier. There are plenty of others elsewhere, so you'll have to get one of those instead."

The dolphin shifters never moved their gazes away from me.

"Your kind isn't welcome in this bar," the largest male said. "Why don't you swim off into the deep."

My smile grew, as did my anger, and I showed them as many of my teeth as I could. "Sorry, corpse fuckers, but I got here first."

"At least we can get laid. Last I heard, your dorsal fin was perfectly smooth," the smallest male said with a cocky grin and a tilt of his head.

Tiger shark males bit the females' dorsal fins when mating. Despite the fact ninety percent of shifters in the world did not mate in animal form, it was one of their favorite insults to use against me.

"I'm just picky about who I fuck," I replied with a shrug of a single shoulder. "I prefer the things I screw to be alive and willing."

The female lunged forward, but ran head first into a

magical barrier that had her face smooshed flat like a glass window. Her nose crunched and she cried out as she fell back.

Jong-hyun sipped from his drink, his eyes glowing yellow, and when he noticed me looking at him, he winked.

Fish nuggets, he was hot.

"Last warning to leave us alone," Grant said and draped his arm around my shoulders. "You're ruining my buzz."

"Just wait until we find you in the waters," the largest male threatened. "Bastian isn't the only one you should be afraid of."

To play off the fear that had my heart hammering in my chest, I scoffed and asked, "You believe that rumor? Even if he were still alive, he wouldn't bother coming here with you peons."

"Oh, he's coming," the middle male said. "I don't expect you to live through the next month. When he takes you, I'll be the first to volunteer to watch him strip you apart piece by piece."

Reed spun up out of his seat, his body partially shifted into wolf form, and slammed his furred fist into the middle male's face, sending him flying across the room and into the backs of two men sitting at the bar.

The two men turned on the dolphin shifter who had hit them and immediately started fighting him.

The dolphin shifters in front of me stood in conflicted silence for a moment, wanting to attack Reed and I, but also wanting to help their friend. Their loyalty to their friend won out, and they ran over to intervene.

"Maybe we should try a different bar?" Jong-hyun suggested.

I nodded in agreement.

The two men who had been sitting at the bar tossed two of the male dolphin shifters backwards, right into a table of college-aged guys.

Within seconds, the entire room was brawling.

"We agree I didn't start this?" I asked. "If that troll bouncer comes, you'll corroborate my story, right?"

The foursome snickered, downed their drinks, and grouped up together at the end of the table, forcing me into the center of them.

"What's going on here?" Pedro, the leader of the local vampire coven bellowed as he stepped into the room.

"Shit," I whispered and ducked my head.

The female dolphin shifter threw a bottle of booze, which sailed over the head of the man she aimed for, and instead, flew straight at Pedro's face. In his shock, he didn't see it until it broke on his cheek.

22

The entire room stilled as Pedro wiped at the broken glass and alcohol now coating his face and upper body.

"Dolphins," Pedro hissed.

"We need to go. Now!" I whisper-hissed into Grant's ear. "He doesn't like me."

Grant nodded once, tilted his head towards the door, and the foursome slowly made their way towards the exit.

Someone had gotten Pedro a towel and he wiped his face off, giving me extra time to escape.

"I can smell you, Shark," Pedro snapped and his head whipped around, his eyes focusing on mine in an instant. "Stop trying to leave."

My body immediately froze.

His eyes turned blood red as he glared at me. "What did you do? Why are you in this bar starting issues?"

"She didn't do anything," Grant retorted. "Those four tried to start a fight they couldn't win."

Pedro's eyes narrowed. "Who are you four? I've never seen you before. Why are you with that ... thing?"

My lips pursed as a snappy retort rushed to the tip of my tongue, but I clenched my teeth together.

"None of your business, vampire. Now, deal with the ones who started the fight and threw a bottle at you, and leave us be," Jong-min snarled.

Pedro crooked his finger at me. "Come here, Shark."

My body was about to move on its own when Jong-min linked his arm through my right arm and Jong-hyun linked his arm through my left arm.

"Let's go," Jong-min whispered.

Fire flared in Pedro's eyes as the twins pulled me away, breaking the power Pedro had over me.

My throat closed and my heart pounded harder in my chest.

"She's not breathing," Jong-hyun whispered.

"Faster. We need to get out of here faster," Grant growled.

Reed, still in half shifted form, howled and suddenly the entire bar parted so we could leave.

My legs grew weak, and I wouldn't have been able to remain upright if it weren't for the twins, who were now carrying me between them.

"Hurry," Jong-hyun gasped. "Hurry."

When this was over, I was going to kill that vampire. I was going to shove a stake through his heart, dick, ass, and down his throat just for good measure.

We rounded a corner, went into an alley, and stopped once the shadows concealed us.

"Hold her," Jong-min snapped.

Grant and Reed took my arms from the twins and shoved me against the wall of the alley.

What were they going to do?

Jong-min and Jong-hyun stepped in front of me, their eyes glowing the same color, and began chanting in a language I didn't understand. No, not chanting ... singing. Moving their hands in a mesmerizing pattern, they wove literal strands of magic in the air, creating a pattern with their combined strands. Jong-min had white magic, while Jong-hyun had black magic. The pattern was intricate, lace-like, and beautiful. It looked like a mandala almost.

The design finished forming, the twins pushed it towards me, and then it wrapped around me from my chest, to my sides, to my back. Once the design connected fully around me, an explosion of magic vibrated through me.

The magic coursed through my system, burning away a dark spot that had been buried within my chest, as well as a dark spot that was in my head.

For a moment, I blacked out, and when I came to, my body was trying to fully shift. I managed to stop it and ended up only shifting my upper body for a second before reverting back to my human form.

"Ouch," I whispered. The only reason I was still upright was because of Grant and Reed holding me. My breaths came in pants as the pain ebbed away.

Jong-min and Jong-hyun blinked, the glow faded from their eyes, and they shook their arms out.

"How do you feel?" Jong-min asked and stepped forward. He set his hand on my upper chest, right above my boobs, and narrowed his eyes.

"Getting a little fresh when you haven't even asked me out on a date yet," I teased.

He rolled his eyes and stepped back. "Obviously she's better if she's speaking like that."

"Can we let go?" Reed asked.

I nodded, but quickly realized they weren't asking me. They were asking Jong-min.

He stared at me a bit longer, his eyes glowed, and then they dimmed and he nodded. "Yes."

"What was that?" I asked. "I ... saw dark spots get burned away."

"The vampire had placed a mark on you," Jong-min answered. "That was why, even though we broke his spell when he ordered you to approach him, you couldn't breathe. Had you run away with Theo or someone else, and they were not able to break the spell, you would have died."

So, they'd dragged me away almost to my demise. If they hadn't been able to break that spell, they would have killed me. Maybe I should have been pissed, but I was really glad not to have that mark on me any longer.

"What was that dark spot in my head?" I asked.

"What?" all four asked simultaneously.

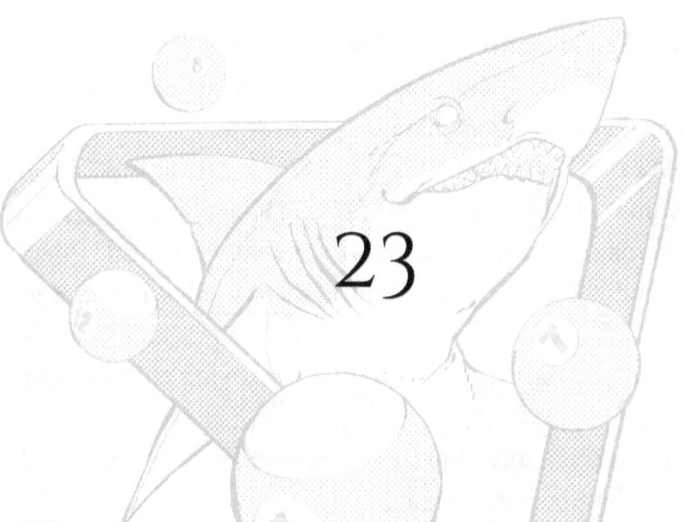

23

"When your magic burned away the dark spot in my chest, it also burned away a dark spot in my head," I said, and tapped my skull.

Jong-min looked at Jong-hyun, who shrugged. Jong-min grabbed Jong-hyun by the shoulder, dragged him further down the alley, and they spoke in hushed, but angry tones, waving their hands around exaggeratedly.

"I can't believe you guys started a bar fight," I said to Reed, smiling wide, and rocked on my heels. "It was pretty hot."

Reed returned my smile with one of his own. "If that vampire hadn't shown up, it would have gotten a whole lot hotter. I was preparing to take the fight downstairs, too."

"You sure you're okay?" Grant asked, scowling.

"I feel great," I admitted, raised my arms, and looked down at myself. "It's like a weight was lifted I didn't even know was there." I jumped and landed lightly on my toes. "I feel so much lighter."

Jong-min and Jong-hyun returned, both with their brows

furrowed and mouths turned down at the ends.

"Those expressions don't instill confidence in me," I mumbled and linked my hands together.

"We don't know what that spot in your head was," Jong-min admitted. "We only saw the one in your chest."

"Perhaps someone else put a mark in your head," Jong-hyun said. "Though, we should have been able to see it as well."

"And you didn't," I summed up. "So, what could it have been?"

"We aren't sure, but our magic cures darkness, so I wouldn't be worried," Jong-min said.

"Cures darkness?" I asked. "That's pretty cool."

"Well, it cleanses the darkness away more than cures it," Jong-hyun said.

"Well, either way ... " I stepped closer to them, bowed, and said, "Thank you."

When I straightened, I saw a new expression on Jong-min's face I hadn't seen before. Was that ... trust? Had I somehow earned a tad more of his trust?

"Since that bar was a bust, do you want to go to Silver's?" Grant asked. "Or would you prefer to head back to our hotel, eat snacks, watch movies, and relax?"

"Relaxing sounds great," I said. "And snacks. I am craving some sugar. Chocolate specifically."

"Let's stop by the convenience store on the way back," Reed said. "I want to get some more pork rinds and soda."

"Perfect! I can get some of my favorite snacks and drinks while we're there to take back to your hotel," I said.

"Are you going to stay over?" Grant asked. "You're welcome to stay on the couch."

I shrugged, spun on my heel, and sashayed my way out of the alley. "We will have to see how the night goes."

"Mm," Reed growled appreciatively behind me. "I'm going to walk back here."

"We can't all walk behind her," Grant mumbled.

"It's your date," Jong-hyun whispered. "So you walk beside her and let the rest of us enjoy the view."

Clutching my stomach, I doubled over in laughter. "You guys are too much! You know I can hear you, right?"

As I continued to laugh, I noticed their cheeks tinted red. Had they not realized I could hear them?

A few blocks of silence later, we made it to the little convenience store that was surprisingly well-stocked.

We walked inside, and I was happy to see it was empty except for the cashier, a tall, thin dhampir who was mindlessly flipping through a magazine, obviously bored. He had a teal and purple mohawk that was at least a foot tall, and wore matching teal and purple eyeshadow that sparkled on his upper eyelids. He glanced up when we came in, dipped his head once, and returned to his magazine.

"Get your favorites," Grant said as he held out one of the plastic shopping baskets.

I took it with a wide smile and hurried off down the aisles. I grabbed my favorite chips, jerky, candy, donuts, pretzels, and muffins, then moved on to juices, energy drinks, and sodas.

I was the last to the counter and when I set my heavy basket down, they all stared at the basket and then at me with wide eyes.

Grant smiled, slid the basket towards the cashier, and asked, "You sure you didn't miss anything?"

Below the register on the front of the counter were some of the most popular candy bars. I grabbed one of the bags of candy-coated chocolate pieces and tossed it into my basket. "Now I'm good."

Jong-hyun let out a bark of laughter and then hurriedly covered his mouth and ducked his head.

More people started to come inside and the shop was small, so I told Grant I'd wait outside for him.

As soon as I was outside, I felt my phone vibrate and pulled it out to see a message from an unknown phone number.

You may have broken my bond, but that won't keep me from finding you. I will ALWAYS find you.

Chills ran down my spine and I read the message over and over again trying to figure out who it was from and what they meant.

It wasn't from Pedro. I knew that because I had his number saved in my phone.

So, who was it from?

Who?

Someone set a hand on my shoulder and I spun, punched them in the stomach, and shifted my head into shark form all in a matter of seconds.

Huffing, I stared at Reed doubled over, clutching his stomach, and the other three guys looking at me with a mixture of wide eyes and furrowed brows.

After swallowing past the lump in my throat, I shifted back and apologized. "Sorry. I'm sorry. You startled me."

"What's got you so spooked?" Jong-min asked.

I didn't know these guys. They *had* protected me against Pedro and removed his mark, though.

"Here," I said and held out my phone, trying to quell the shaking of my hand.

Jong-min took the phone and the other three stood around him to read over his shoulders.

"Who sent it?" Jong-min asked.

I shook my head. "I don't know."

"This must have been that spot in her head she mentioned," Jong-hyun whispered.

"You sure it wasn't the vampire?" Reed asked, his voice slightly deeper and with a hint of a growl.

"I have Pedro's number saved in my phone," I explained. "So, it couldn't be from him."

They gave me disapproving looks.

"Don't judge," I snapped.

"Let's get to the room," Grant said. "We can talk more there."

"Yeah, I don't like being out in the open right now," I admitted.

Reed took the bags from Grant and I wasn't sure why until Grant draped his arm around my shoulders and tugged me against his side.

"It'll be alright. We will go inside and figure this out together. Okay?" he whispered as we started walking towards the hotel.

"This really isn't your guys' problem. I don't want to put you in unnecessary danger," I whispered back. "I can just leave. No hard feelings." Despite saying that, the thought of leaving to go off by myself made my chest hurt. I couldn't go to Theo's, because I didn't want to bring danger to her, either.

Maybe it was time for me to leave this city. Maybe it was time for me to return to the sea.

"You're not putting us in any unnecessary danger. We want to continue our date and learn more about you," he replied instantly. "If you want to leave because you don't want to see where this goes, that's one thing, but if you want to leave to try to protect us, you can just flush that thought right out of your head."

"I don't think you guys are weak, or anything. We just don't know each other and—"

"And that's why we're on this date," he interrupted me. He squeezed my arm and smiled. "Come on, beautiful, don't cut my date off yet. If you end my date early, the others will tease me."

They wouldn't tease him, but I could tell what he was trying to do and I appreciated it.

"Alright, but if we get attacked, Jong-min can't get mad at me and try to blame me," I said loud enough for the cat shifter to hear.

Jong-min muttered something beneath his breath too low for me to hear, but I could tell it wasn't flattering.

We waited at the crosswalk to make the last steps to the hotel. There were several others around us, most in pairs or groups, many intoxicated already.

Two pops sounded, and I had just started to duck when everyone started screaming in fear.

Grant picked me up and calmly walked across the street and into the hotel, dodging all of the terrified people.

I looked up at him and my mouth fell open.

Grant had shifted part of his face so that it was covered in dragon scales. Two bullets were lodged in the side of his face, stuck in the scales.

"You ... you're shot," I whispered.

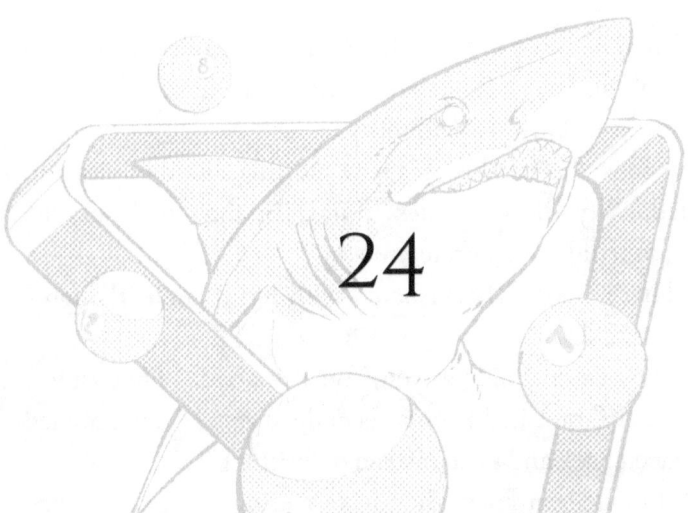

24

"I'm fine," he said. Or, I'm pretty sure that's what he said. He sounded mostly like a dragon, full of fire and growl.

Instead of taking the elevator, he took the stairs. I could have walked, but he seemed to be in full defense mode, and I felt it was best to just stay quietly in his arms until we got into the room. Also, the other three weren't freaking out as they walked behind us, so that had to mean they weren't worried about Grant.

How they weren't worried about him being shot in the face *twice*, I didn't know, but I just kept tamping down my fear.

As soon as we got into the hotel room, Jong-min and Jong-hyun set up protection barriers and did some other spell I'd never seen before that formed a red wall in front of the window.

Grant stood in the center of the living room, holding me in his arms while they worked, and only put me down once they were finished.

When he put me down, he reached out and brushed the bullets off his face, letting them clatter to the floor.

"Are you okay?" I asked softly.

He looked at me, his eyes now sporting slitted pupils, and nodded. "My dragon scales formed in time to block the bullet, so it didn't penetrate my skin."

"That's handy," I whispered with a soft smile, though I felt is shake slightly.

"They were aiming at you," Reed snarled. "They almost got you. If Grant had been a second slower ... " He growled and paced back and forth instead of finishing his sentence.

"How do you know they were aiming for me?" I asked softly, fear making my throat tight.

"I had to duck so the bullet would hit me instead of you," Grant replied, his voice, and eyes, finally back to normal.

"Y-you ... what? Wait. You purposefully ducked *into* the bullet?" I asked, my mouth barely not hanging open.

He nodded. "I couldn't let it hit you. I wasn't sure your skin was strong enough to stop a bullet."

"It isn't," I admitted.

"Who would try to kill you?" Jong-min asked, his arms folded across his chest.

"I don't know anyone who wants to kill me. Sure, I tick off a lot of people, but they're just angry with me, not to the point of wanting to murder me." My butt hit the couch and I let my head fall into my hands.

Jong-hyun had gone into the adjoining room, but came back in with his phone up to his ear. "No, she's fine. We're keeping her here, and I don't think it's a good idea for you to walk about in the open right now either; not until we figure out who shot at her and sent her the message. We think they might be connected, but we don't have concrete evidence of that yet."

"Who are you talking to?" I demanded and jumped to my feet, racing to snatch the phone from him.

He held out the phone. "Theo."

I took it and sucked in a breath before quickly saying, "I have no idea what's going on, or who it could be. We got into a scuffle with the dolphins and Pedro was there, but this isn't his style. Though they did discover the bastard had marked me."

"I thought I'd sensed something, but it was so faint I wasn't sure," Theo grumbled. "What is this about something in your head?"

"When they did the cleansing spell thing, I felt a dark spot in my head being cleaned away, too. I didn't know it was there before and have no idea where it came from or what it was. I'm assuming whoever sent me that message was the person who did that."

"I've felt that spot before. It felt like a memory block," Theo admitted.

"And you never told me!" I shouted.

"I didn't want to risk you getting hurt more by knowing it was there. Some memory spells can irreparably injure the person if they know they are there," she explained.

"I'm sorry," I exhaled. "I didn't mean to snap at you. I'm just stressing out."

"To be expected when someone just tried to assassinate you," she said, and I could tell she was smiling. "I think it is best if you stay the night with them tonight."

"You just want me to get laid," I muttered as quietly as I could. Judging by the few chuckles behind me, I wasn't quiet enough.

"You do need to get laid," she agreed. "Seriously, though, I think they can protect you as well as I could, and I don't want you walking around in the open to come to my place."

"I can't freaking hide for the rest of my life," I snapped.

"No, but maybe you can figure out who is after you before tomorrow," she said softly. Her voice dropped and there was so much emotion in her next sentences that I felt myself choke up. "Stay safe, okay? I can't lose you."

I swallowed hard. "Yes, ma'am. You stay safe, too. Who knows if they might come after you next?"

"I wish a motherfucker would," she snapped.

Laughter bubbled up out of me, and I smiled wide. She always knew how to make me smile, even in the worst circumstances. "Love you."

"Love you, too. Now hand me back to that adorable twin."

I held the phone out to Jong-hyun, who took it and walked back into the other room.

With a sigh, I sat back on the couch and tried to think who could be the cause of this new threat. Who would want to kill me?

"Oh fuck," I whispered and stood as a thought occurred to me. I reached into my pocket and pulled out the business card the hunter had given me.

"What?" Grant asked, and looked over my shoulder to see what I was holding. "Is that the hunter's card?"

"What if ... " I didn't even want to voice the thought out loud.

"What?" Grant pushed.

"What if it's Bastian?" I asked in the softest whisper.

25

"Fuck," Reed growled and walked to the closet, where he opened a large suitcase on the floor.

"Triple the barriers!" Jong-min yelled to Jong-hyun through the open door between the shared rooms.

"We don't have enough supplies," Reed yelled as he rifled through the large suitcase.

"Shouldn't we have felt his magic?" Grant asked the others.

"Yes, but he could have sent the triplets ahead," Jong-hyun answered from the other room.

"That could explain why you got shot," Reed said, pulling small vials of different colored liquids out. "They could have been trying to shoot her through you, not caring if they killed you, too."

"Whoa!" I yelled. "What are you all talking about? You know him? What is going on?"

"Let's fortify our defenses, and then we can talk," Grant said. "Kass, sit down on the couch, please."

I sat, feeling nervous and terrified all at once. The ocean was sounding better and better each minute that went by.

My phone chimed, and the four of them rushed over, crowding around me as I unlocked the screen.

Come willingly, or I'll slaughter them. Meet me at the pier tomorrow at dawn.

"Fuck," I whispered. It had to be him. There was no one else who would message in such a way. "How did he get my number? How the fuck did he find me? Fuck. Fuck!"

Grant snatched the phone out of my hand and started typing a reply.

"What are you doing? Are you fucking insane!" I tried to grab the phone back, but Reed snaked his arm around my waist and pulled me back against his chest.

"Deep breath," Reed whispered. "We've got this."

"No, you don't! You have no idea what that insane megalomaniac is capable of. Don't respond to him. Don't engage. I have to leave. I need to get as far from here as possible, or—"

"It's too late," Grant said. His eyes were full of worry as he said, "He's already here, Kass. It's too late to run."

That's where he was wrong. I could run. Not to escape, but to draw Bastian away from the foursome, and protect them from his wrath.

"Give me my phone back," I said as calmly as possible, and held out my hand.

"No," all four responded simultaneously.

"I need to message Theo." Maybe if I explained it calmly to them, they'd understand.

"No, you're going to try to reason with him. He cannot be reasoned with," Jong-min said.

"You can't respond to him on my behalf. You are not my

mates." Despite saying it calmly, it came off really harsh and cruel.

After a moment of tense silence, Grant turned to face me.

"No, we aren't your mates, but we aren't going to let you kill yourself to protect us, either," Grant said.

"I'm not going to kill myself," I said, and rolled my eyes.

"We'll buy you a new phone," Grant said.

My brows furrowed. A new phone? Was he really just going to hold the phone forever?

Scales covered his hand, and before I could even open my mouth, he squeezed and the phone was immediately crushed. Pieces fell to the ground as my mouth fell open.

"Y-you crushed it!" I squeaked.

He brushed some of the pieces off his hand and held out my sim card. "Here."

"If he is after her, maybe we can use that to our advantage," Jong-min said.

Reed growled and his lip pulled up in a snarl.

Jong-min raised his hands. "Okay, forget I suggested it."

"Let's just relax and watch some funny movies," Grant suggested. "He and his minions can't get in here, and there's no reason to stress about shit we can't control."

Grant and Reed sat on either side of me on the couch while Jong-min and Jong-hyun sat on the opposite couch, just like last time.

"How do you guys know him?" I asked, still not yet at ease.

"We used to live in a coastal area and he had the nerve to show up there. Luckily, the packs that lived there were land shifters and he had no interest in them. He still left a bad taste in our mouths and after some research, we found out about him and how disgusting he was. So, the brothers went to great lengths to prepare countermeasures should we ever encounter him again," Grant explained.

I leaned back against the couch and tried my best to relax. Bastian was likely going to wait until I was alone to visit me, now that the shooter had failed, and he knew I was with people who could protect me.

Grant draped an arm around my shoulders, and I leaned into him, letting his body heat warm me. I'd always found it odd that in my shark form I preferred the cold, while in my human form I preferred to be hot. He shifted even closer to me, until our legs were touching from hip to knee and my upper body was partially on top of his chest.

At the earliest opportunity, I needed to find the Chums and warn them that Bastian was here, so they could flee.

Absentmindedly, I grabbed snacks and ate, not really tasting the food or hearing the movie.

Reed set a hand on my knee and rubbed his thumb across it. Shifters were big on touch in general, and I wasn't sure if he was trying to console me or himself by touching me. I didn't mind either way.

With Grant and Reed both touching me, the fear and craziness of the day finally hit me, and since I felt safe with them, I started to doze.

My head started to fall forward, waking me, and my eyes snapped open.

The couch where the twins had been was empty, the television was turned off, and yet I was still squished between Reed and Grant.

Grant gently pushed my head back so it lay on his

shoulder and then draped his arm around my stomach. "It's okay. You're safe. Go back to sleep."

"Bathroom," I whispered, and licked my dry lips.

He detangled himself from around me, but when I tried to stand, Reed latched onto me with a soft growl.

"Gotta pee," I whispered to him.

Reed mumbled something in his sleep and let me go.

After using the bathroom and washing my hands, I stared in the mirror at myself. For years, I'd been safe from Bastian. His memory just that, a memory. Now, he was back and I had no doubts that he was here to finish what he'd started a decade ago.

With a deep breath, I shoved my fear down and returned to the living room. Reed and Grant were both gone, the room empty.

26

My brows furrowed, and I looked at the kitchen to see if they were in there, but that was empty as well.

Was I dreaming? Was this a hallucination? They wouldn't have left me, right? Had they destroyed the phone because they'd worked out a deal to give me over to Bastian to save themselves, and hadn't wanted me to see the text reply they'd sent? Had they sold me out to save themselves? That would be fitting and in line with the rest of my life and experiences.

Warm hands slid around my waist as I stared at the empty couch and pulled me back against an even warmer body. "What's got your heart racing?" Grant asked in a soft whisper against my neck.

Relief flooded me, and I sagged against him slightly, feeling guilty for thinking they'd sold me out. "I thought you might have abandoned me to Bastian," I admitted.

He stepped around me and tilted my chin up with his fingertips. Fire glowed within his eyes as he stared into mine. "We would never do that." His fingers slid along my jaw, featherlight, and the fire changed slightly. "You're fucking beautiful, Kass. So beautiful, it makes me wonder if this is all a dream."

Pushing up onto my tiptoes, I pressed my lips to his. "If it is a dream, I hope we never wake up," I whispered against his lips.

His arms wound around me, and he kissed me back, his tongue sliding along the seam of my lips. I opened to him willingly, wrapped my arms around his waist, and slid my hands up his muscular back.

His tongue danced with mine as he walked us back to the couch. He sat down, and I sat on his lap, my arms around his neck and chest pressed to his as we continued to kiss.

Starfish, he was an amazing kisser!

His erection grew between us, and I adjusted my position so I could grind against him.

He moaned into my mouth and his hands slid down to grip my ass, kneading the muscles with his fingers.

A second pair of hands slid around my stomach and up to cup my breasts, thumbs stroking across my nipples.

I broke our kiss, turned my head, and Reed immediately kissed me, his tongue hot and demanding.

Grant began slowly moving his hips to match my movements, increasing the friction even more. He leaned forward and kissed my upper chest while Reed continued to devour my mouth.

My throaty moan was swallowed by Reed's mouth and I could feel that I had soaked my underwear and through my pants.

"Why don't we take this to the room?" Grant suggested.

I nodded and licked my swollen lips. "Yes, please."

Grant picked me up and carried me to the bedroom, setting me down on the end of the bed. He stepped back and I watched as he and Reed both stripped out of their clothes.

"Dinner and a show. This is the best date ever."

Reed laughed, grabbed my hands, and pulled me up to my feet.

Grant stepped behind me, slide his hands along my stomach so he could grip the hem of my shirt, and pulled it up over my head.

Within moments, I was naked before them.

"So beautiful," Reed praised before taking my mouth again.

Reed's right hand cupped my face a moment, then his fingers skimmed down my sides, around my front, and dipped into my warm, dripping core.

He pulled back, eyes wide as he stared down at me. "You're so wet."

Grant kissed my upper back and pressed his erection against me. "She smells delicious."

Reed slid his fingers out and dropped to his knees, immediately burying his face and licking me. "She tastes even better," he said, only pulling back long enough to say those words before he continued licking me.

"Yes!" I breathed, leaning back against Grant with closed eyes.

Reaching back, I gripped Grant and started slowly working his shaft.

"Open your eyes," Grant ordered me.

Reed suddenly stopped and stood. "Let's get comfortable."

Grant nodded and guided me back to the bed.

Before they could choose the position for me, I shoved Grant backwards, his back hit the mattress, and his eyes widened, likely not remembering I was strong.

I crawled across the bed, between his legs, and licked the head of his penis where a drop of precum glistened.

Reed lay on his back and slid up until his face was even with my hips, then angled my hips down so he could resume eating me.

I moaned and dropped forward, taking Grant in until he hit the back of my throat.

He moaned and closed eyes his a moment.

Slowly, I relaxed my throat and took the rest of him, glad I didn't have a gag reflex, and glad I was able to keep my teeth back.

"Fuck," he hissed and gripped my hair.

My orgasm hit out of nowhere, making me buck against Reed's face, but he held my hips, licking faster and harder through it.

I squirted a tad, the juices leaking down my legs, but Reed licked them clean before sliding out from beneath me.

"Oh, gods, Grant, she's a squirter."

Grant looked down at me and I winked as I increased my pace, swallowing him all the way to the base and swirling my tongue around his head when I pulled back.

Reed put on a condom, raised my hips up, and slowly slid into me.

He was decent-sized, but I was able to accommodate him without more foreplay.

He gripped my hips and set a hard and fast pace that forced me to stop with Grant, fearful I might accidently nick him with a tooth when I orgasmed. I licked from his base all the way to the tip.

Reed hit the perfect spot, tearing an orgasm out of me that had me squirting so much that I soaked him.

I held back my scream, not wanting to wake the twins in the other room.

Reed continued his merciless pace, but it wasn't long before he finished. "She's so wet and squeezes hard when she comes."

Grant grabbed a condom and patted Reed's shoulder. "It happens to us all, bro."

I snickered, breathless, and rolled onto my back. Reed lay down beside me, turned my head, and kissed me.

Grant leaned down and took one of my nipples into his mouth as he slowly entered me. He was larger than Reed, but I was so wet it only took him a few strokes to get fully sheathed within me.

Reed kneaded one of my breasts while Grant set a slow, hard pace that I could feel building my orgasm already.

Grant increased his pace a bit more and I screamed into Reed's mouth as I orgasmed.

Grant leaned back, raised my hips a bit, and quickened his pace more, our bodies slamming together in a delicious sound and feel.

A normal girl might have bruised, but I wasn't normal.

Something warm blossomed in my chest, I reached out, setting a hand on Grand and Reed, the sensation grew until it was almost unbearable, and then disappeared.

Reed pulled back from our kiss, eyes golden. "I want to watch your face the next time you come."

He didn't have to wait long. Grant found the perfect

angle that stroked right along my g-spot. I bit my lower lip to keep from screaming and my eyes rolled up into my head.

Grant shuddered above me, finishing as well, and fell to his side beside me.

My body felt boneless as the three of us lay together, sweat coating our skin, and satisfaction making us all smile.

"Shower?" I asked, still panting.

Grant picked me up and carried me against his chest into the bathroom. Reed followed behind us, turned on the water in the shower, and pulled out shampoo and soap from beneath the sink.

The shower was average-sized for a hotel, which meant this shower was going to be cramped. And I was *totally* okay with that.

Reed stepped in, his hand in the spray of water as he waited for it to warm up. Once the water was warm enough, Reed nodded once.

Grant set me on my feet in the shower and climbed in right behind me. Once again, I was squashed between the dragon and wolf shifters, and I found I enjoyed this predicament.

They worked methodically, and it became apparent that this wasn't their first time sharing a shower together. I had known through our time earlier that they had shared a woman before, but now it was once again apparent.

"Do you always share your women?" I asked as I shampooed my hair.

"Yes," they answered simultaneously.

Strangely, I felt no jealousy hearing the admission.

"Do you often sleep with multiple men at once?" Grant asked as he began to rub the soap across my upper back.

"No. I've done it twice before, but it's not common for me."

"Did you enjoy your time with us?" Reed asked, looking down at me as he rinsed the shampoo from his hair.

I smirked. "Yes. I figured my squirting and the wet spot on the bed were evidence of that."

Both chuckled and we finished the rest of our shower in silence.

Dressed in a pair of sweats from Reed and a shirt from Grant, I climbed into Grant's bed, the one without a wet spot, and draped myself across the dragon.

Reed climbed in behind me and wrapped an arm around my waist.

"Do you usually sleep together?" I asked sleepily.

"No," Reed mumbled into my hair. "I just wanted to be close to you for a little longer. Do you want me to leave?"

"No, please stay," I whispered, and arched my butt a bit so he could spoon himself around me more easily.

Grant made a sound that was close to a purr and I kissed his bare chest.

"Thank you," I whispered.

"We should definitely be thanking you," Grant whispered back, and kissed the top of my head. "What do you want for breakfast?"

"Biscuits and gravy," I answered sleepily. "With sausage."

"We got plenty of sausage," Reed mumbled, half asleep.

I snorted once, the extent of my available energy.

27

The sun started to rise and my internal clock woke me.

It was time.

Grant and Reed were still wrapped around me, and I debated just staying with them. What if they could protect me? What if they could keep me and Theo safe from Bastian?

No, I couldn't risk it.

I kissed Grant's chest, extricated myself from Reed's hold and kissed his cheek. On silent feet, I made my way out of the room where the two slept like the dead.

Tiptoeing, I made my way to the living room, where I grabbed my ID and clothes, slipped them on, and tied my shoes tight. Then, I grabbed the little notepad the hotel provided by the phone, wrote them a note, and stood before the door.

The twins were sleeping in a bed in the other hotel room, but as soon as I broke their barrier to leave, they would wake. I had to break through and run as fast as I could.

With a deep breath, I reached through their barrier, grabbed the door handle, pulled it open, and ran out. Their power pressed down onto me like a heavy blanket, but I went as fast as possible and ran to the stairs.

I was down two flights before I heard their voices above.

Down, down, down, I went, out the front door, and down the street towards the pier.

At the end of the pier stood a single figure, looking out at the ocean.

In ten years, he hadn't changed at all. Still tall, thin, and regal, appearing exactly like the king he wanted to be. His long brown hair was tied back with a leather strap, his silver eyes as haunting as I remembered.

"I didn't think you'd be able to escape them," he said, his voice carrying on the dawn wind.

Shivering, and not from the cold, I took the last dozen steps to reach him. "They have nothing to do with us. I just met them."

He turned and smiled down at me. "I'm surprised you made friends at all, Sharkling."

"Why are you here? What do you want?" I demanded and folded my arms across my chest.

"I was thwarted before, my power base taken from me. That's not going to happen again. Mistakes were made, some by me, and I will rectify them. My biggest mistake was you." He stepped closer to me. "You weren't a simple shifter like I had thought. Losing you was a huge blow to me, and I didn't realize why for several years. Now, I know. Someone broke my bond with you, but it can be built again. Stronger. Better."

"I don't want to create a bond with you," I snarled, and felt my face shifting. "I want you to fucking die!"

Trying to punch him proved completely pointless as he dodged my fist, stepped around me, and wrapped his arms around my upper body and stomach, holding me like a lover would. It reminded me of the time I'd had with Grant and Reed just hours earlier, and I wanted to tear Bastian apart.

"I know you hate me, and that is something I must atone for. Something I must make up to you. You are to be my queen, Kassidy. You will rule at my side," he whispered into my ear.

"Never!" I snapped and felt my head shift even more.

"You slept with them?" he growled with his nose pressed to my hair. "I'm going to kill them. No one is to touch you. I warned them. I warned them all that you were not to be touched."

"I am not yours!" I bellowed, grabbed his arm, raised it, and bit it off with a jerk of my head.

When I turned, I expected to see anger, fear, pain, something.

Instead, I only saw sadness on Bastian's face. "You will learn that you are meant to be with me. It is our destiny, Kassidy."

"Fuck you!" I shouted. "You almost killed me. You killed my friends."

"You don't have friends, and never will. It is not in your personality to be able to keep friends," he said, as though it were common knowledge, and something I should know.

"I have friends," I said, though my voice wasn't as strong as before. "I am not alone. Not anymore."

"Come with me, and I will spare them all," he whispered. His stump of an arm was still bleeding, a puddle so large that it spilled down the wooden planks and into the sea, attracting true sharks from around the area.

"Leave me the fuck alone, or I will kill you," I said calmly. "Last warning."

"I can tell you need a night to think about it," he said and shrugged. "I will give you until dawn tomorrow to come."

"If you wanted me alive, why send your minions to shoot me?" I asked.

"They acted without knowing my true intent. They have been punished for attempting to kill you. Had they succeeded, my wrath would have leveled this city," he said. His eyes glowed, and the pier's wooden boards quaked beneath our feet. "No one will kill you. Never."

"Leave this city and never return," I ordered him. "I do not want to see you in my city ever again."

"Tomorrow. Dawn. Don't be late," he said, and with a snap of his fingers he disappeared.

"Kass!" four male voices yelled.

My knees finally gave out and I fell to my butt, staring at my hands, which shook in my lap.

I had known he was insane, but now he was trying to claim me as his, which marked him as even crazier.

"Kass," Grant whispered and reached towards me.

I leaped up and backed towards the end of the pier. "Stay away from me. You're in danger near me."

"What did he say?" Jong-min asked.

"Tell Theo I'm sorry," I whispered and swallowed hard. "I'm so sorry."

With a deep breath, I leaped over the end of the pier, shifted into my full shark form, and swam down into the cool depths of the ocean.

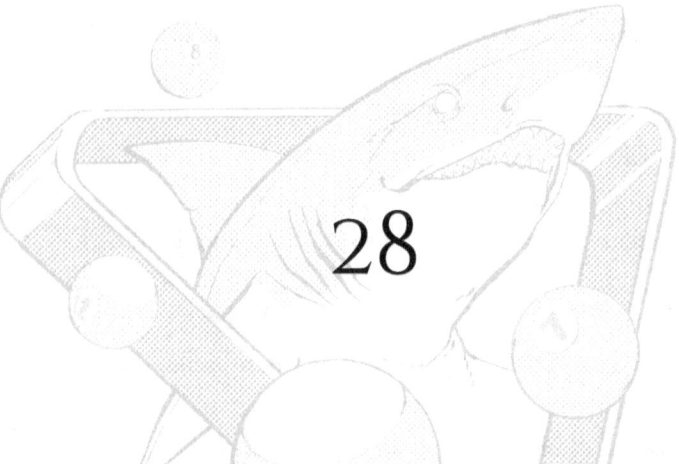

28

The cold waters of the ocean surrounded me. Deeper and deeper I swam, farther and farther away from humanity.

Out here, it didn't matter if I was liked. If I had friends or not. If I had love or not. If there was a psycho after me or not.

All that mattered out here was eating and surviving.

My mind drifted like the current I swam on.

Swim, breathe, eat.

Swim, breathe, eat.

A creature swam above me, legs and arms moving.

Creature? Edible?

Or human?

To find out required biting. Biting could kill if it was human. Humans tasted terrible. Humans tasted like sadness, regret, and chemicals.

I hated them.

Turning, I returned to my main location, a sunken ship that had settled at the bottom of the sea and was now covered in sea life. The ship had holes in the sides that allowed me to swim inside and hide while dozing. It also provided me a great spot for ambushing fish, crabs, and other tasty morsels.

Round and round the ship I swam, my humanity slowly drifting away.

Water. Water. Fish. Crab!

A giant octopus swam towards me, and I immediately went on the defensive, preparing to chase it away from my new home.

The octopus shifted into a human male, his mouth moved, and he waved his arms at me.

Instead of biting him, I slammed my tail against his body, sending him careening away from my ship.

He held his hands up in surrender, but continued trying to talk to me.

With a snap of my jaws right by his hand, he finally gave up, shaking his head, and swam away.

That's right, this is my territory. You better leave!

The time ebbed and flowed like the waves, the sunlight barely able to reach this far down. I only knew a day had passed when the sun changed twice. My brain had stopped trying to keep track of the number of times it had changed, though, so I had no idea how long I'd been back at sea.

Who needed to track such things? Definitely not a shark.

Sharks only needed food. And sex, but sex didn't sound good. Not with the sharks here.

An image of human men's faces crossed my mind and I quickly shook it away.

No! I was a shark. No humans. Humans were bad. Humans, bad.

More shifters tried to invade my home, tried to communicate with me, but I would not be bartered with. They could find their own places.

Three more shifters came: a squid, a seal, and a dolphin. They tried to forcibly restrain me, but I showed them I was not to be trifled with. The dolphin almost didn't survive, which would have been fine with me. Dolphin meat was delicious.

Finally, the shifter bastards left me alone, and I swam alone around the shipwreck.

For some reason, being alone made me both sad and happy at the same time. Why would I be sad? What use was sadness to a shark?

No matter how hard I tried to ignore the sadness, it pressed against me like a brand. I wanted it to go away, but I didn't want to leave my ship. No, this was my home.

I wouldn't leave my home.

Food.

Swim.

Food.

Swim.

Swim.

A storm raged overhead, forcing me to swim lower and closer to the ship.

Four sharks swam towards me, their fins scarred and one had a giant hook through his dorsal fin. The one with the hook also had a hat atop his head and I wondered how he managed to keep it on despite the raging sea.

Snapping my jaws, I warned them to stay away from my shipwreck, my home, but they ignored me, continuing to swim circles around me.

Slowly, recognition hit.

I knew them. My human brain recognized them, while my shark brain only recognized they weren't enemies.

They swam in circles around me, forcing me to slow.

The shark with the hat stopped in front of me, shifted partially, and pointed up.

He wanted me to swim to the surface.

The surface had lots of dangers. Like ... *him*.

I tried to swim away, but the other sharks stopped me.

I could have fought them. I could have killed them, but something stopped me. Some part of me didn't want to hurt these sharks.

Reluctantly, I swam to the top, keeping an eye on the other sharks with him to ensure they weren't planning to ambush me.

Once at the surface, all of the others partially shifted, so I did as well, though it took me a few minutes longer than it should have.

"Wh-what?" I asked, my voice strange since I hadn't used it recently.

"You need to return," the one with the hat, who I remembered was called Cap'n, said.

"R-return? I am a shark in the ocean. I belong here. This is h-home. I'm supp-supposed to be here. I am a shark in the ocean," I said quickly, cursing myself silently for stuttering so much, but it was hard for the words to form.

"Shit. She's been in shark form too long," one of them said.

"You need to return to the city," Cap'n said.

"Why? Why should I go to a human city? Humans are trash. Why should I go near them?" I asked, and crossed my arms over my chest as I continued to kick my feet to stay afloat. I realized the storm had settled and wondered if it was a coincidence or a premonition.

"Your friends are in danger. If you don't return, they'll likely be killed," Cap'n said.

Friends? I didn't have friends. I was a shark. A predator. A loner.

"Follow us," Cap'n said.

"How do we jog her memories?" one of the other sharks asked.

"They'll return as she gets closer to shore," Cap'n said.

"We have to hurry," another of the sharks said. "We need to get her back soon, or all will be lost."

29

"Don't fret, we will get her back in time," Cap'n said. He turned to me, narrowed his eye, and ordered, "Shift to shark form and follow us. We need to get you back to the city as soon as possible. Do not argue with me. We are allies, and I need to take you to this place as soon as possible."

"No," I said firmly. "I live there. I am a shark and that is my home." I pointed down to the shipwreck.

He shook his head. "That is not your home. Technically, that is my ship and my property, so you are trespassing. The only reason I'm not there is because we made a better life on land. A life made better because you were there and you helped us. We need you to help us again. We need you, Kass."

"Land is bad," I whispered. The longer I talked, the longer I stayed in human form, the more of my memories that started to return. I shoved them down as I felt pain coming with them, though. I didn't want to see these. I didn't want to remember the things about my past. It was the past and needed to stay there, while I lived here and now in the seas and just ate and swam. That was what sharks did: ate and swam.

"Child, I have known you many years. Please, trust this old shark. Please, come with me," Cap'n said, his eyes pleading.

For some reason, I trusted him. I gave him a nod before shifting back into my full shark form and following him and the others.

We swam for what felt like days, only stopping to feed on occasion, and no matter what we faced, they stayed with me.

Why were these sharks being friendly to me with no chance of breeding? Was this a common thing? Had I forgotten this was common with them?

Closer we swam towards the shore where the humans lived, and I felt my unease continuing to grow.

If it weren't for the allies around me, urging me on, I would have stopped and fled.

Why were they leading me this way? What lay ahead that I had to see?

There was darkness that way. Darkness and pain. I was certain of it.

I stopped several miles from shore and shifted, forcing them to shift and surface as well. "That's bad!" I said and pointed towards shore.

"There is bad there," Cap'n agreed with a nod. "But you must go. You must face the darkness to let the light back."

"That's stupid! I shouldn't have come. The sea is my home. The sea loves me," I shouted.

"You must come back," one of the other sharks said. "They're going to kill her if you don't come."

Her?

"Who?" I asked softly. While I didn't like the idea of going that way, something was tingling in the back of my brain.

"Your best friend," the shark said. "Theo."

Theo? Theo? Theo?

The name repeated in my head over and over and a face popped into my vision. A kind woman with magic who took scared, little shark me in. The one who took care of me when I had been left for dead.

"She needs you," Cap'n said. "We all need you. You are the only one who can help us right now. Please."

I shook my head and swam backwards. "Death. That way is death."

"Plan B?" the largest shark asked.

Cap'n sighed and nodded. "Aye."

Before I could react, the three sharks with the captain converged on me and knocked me unconscious.

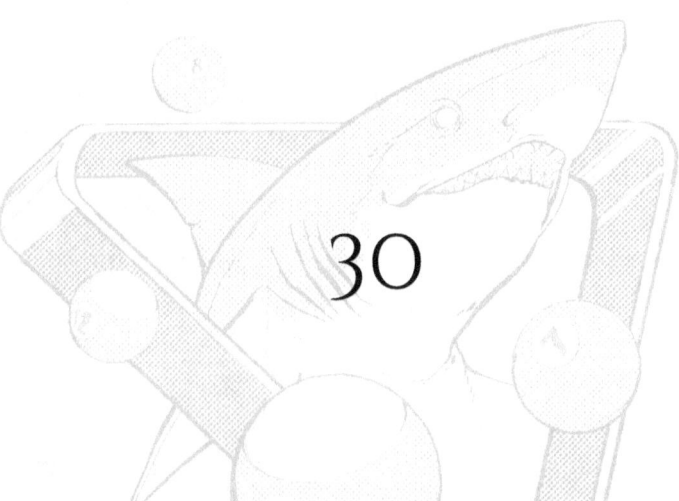

30

A large turtle swam around me, eyeing me nervously.

When had I gotten into the aquarium tank? It felt like years had passed since I'd last been here.

Children walked around the aquarium and I swam slowly, not eating, as I wasn't hungry. Not yet, at least.

I swam for my full work shift, climbed out once all of the visitors were gone, and quickly dressed.

Four men approached me and I tensed, ready to fight. Two of the men were obviously twins, but all four were pleasing to the eyes.

"Kass?" one asked, and took a step towards me.

"Who are you?" I demanded and took a step back. "What do you want?"

"Fuck, Cap'n Two-teeth wasn't kidding," one of the twins whispered.

"How do you know Cap?" I asked and relaxed slightly. If they knew the Chums, they likely weren't bad people.

"Kass, you don't recognize us at all?" one of the men asked. He was the least attractive of the group in the face, but for some reason, I knew, or assumed, he had a really good body. And assumed he was a good kisser.

"Should I?" I asked softly. "I'm sorry. Sometimes I go on benders and black out."

The most attractive one stomped up to me, bent down, and kissed me, stroking my tongue with his. His warm body wrapped around mine and I felt ... safe.

Reed.

Reed!

His name was Reed!

I jumped up, wrapped my arms around his neck, and my legs around his waist while still kissing him.

He broke the kiss and smiled down at me. "You remember?"

"Reed," I whispered. "You're Reed."

He nodded and rested his forehead against mine. "Yes."

I turned and held my hand out to Grant. He immediately came over and stole me from Reed, burying his face in my hair right behind my ear.

"Grant," I whispered.

"Kass," he whispered back and swallowed hard. "Dammit, Kass, where have you been?"

"I-I don't know," I admitted and scowled.

"We tossed her in the tank last night, hoping it would jog her memories," Cap'n Two-teeth said as he and his men walked into the back.

"What?" I asked.

Grant set me on my feet, but kept an arm around me, a hand on my stomach.

"Theo is in trouble, Kass," Jong-min said softly. "We tried to save her, but he won't give her up without seeing you first."

"He?" I asked, and staggered. I would have fallen to my knees if Grant hadn't had ahold of me, pulling me back against his body. All of my memories returned in a rush and I gasped. "Fuck. Fuck. Fuck."

"He has Theo," Grant whispered in my ear.

"He has hidden so well that none of us can find him," a new voice said.

We all turned to look at the hunter from before.

"How did you all find me?" I snapped. "How did any of you know about this place?"

"Let's leave and talk somewhere else," the hunter suggested. "We don't want any of the humans involved."

"We can't take her out into the public without filling her in. He could have people waiting for her to show up," Reed snarled.

The hunter sighed. "True."

"Spill it," I snapped. "Everything. Tell me everything that has happened since I left. How long have I even been gone?"

"A month," Reed whispered, and there was no mistaking the pain in his voice.

A month? I'd been out at sea for a month? That explained why I hadn't been able to access my human memories.

"Maybe we should find somewhere to sit?" Grant suggested, feeling me sag against him again.

"Follow me," I said, pulled away from him, and led the group to the café, which was empty since the aquarium was closed for the day.

Instead of sitting in one of the chairs, I sat on top of one of the tables and crossed my legs.

The others took seats around me, forming a semicircle.

"You left, and for the first few days everything was fine,"

Grant whispered. "He said he wanted to give you time to consider his proposal."

"What was his proposal?" the hunter asked.

My hands clenched in my lap and I snarled. "There was no proposal. Just a demand. He thinks we are meant to be together. That I'm supposed to be his queen and rule by his side. He thinks he lost before because he lost me."

Reed and Grant growled simultaneously.

"That explains a lot," the hunter whispered.

"What if he is right?" Jong-hyun asked.

Jong-min slapped the back of his head. "You going to hand her over to him? Use her to save your skin? I thought you were smarter than that."

"I wasn't suggesting we hand her over," Jong-hyun said as he rubbed the back of his head. "I was just wondering if perhaps he was right. If he is, we need to keep her somewhere safe so that he cannot touch her."

"I have to go to him," I said and slid off the table. "I need to rescue Theo. Where is he?"

"I can't let you do that," the hunter said, stood, and stepped in my path.

Immediately, everyone in the room partially shifted and surrounded us.

"You can't stop me," I whispered to him. "If I have to incapacitate you, I will, but I don't want to. Just let me rescue my friend. I hate him with every ounce of my being. I bit off half his arm the last time I saw him. This time, I will end it. I'll kill him, or he will kill me. Those are the only outcomes. Besides, he seems to be able to keep tabs on most of you and hide from you. Otherwise, you wouldn't have scoured the ocean for me."

"You don't have to fight him alone," Grant said. "You aren't alone anymore."

"That's where you're wrong," I whispered without turning to face them, my heart already constricting. "I am alone, and always will be. It was a mistake for me to make a home here. To make friends that I put in harm's way. I will save Theo. I will kill *him*. Then, I will return to the ocean, where I belong."

Without meeting any of their eyes, I walked out of the café, out of the building, and headed towards the place I suspected he was likely at.

"Wait," Zyra snapped as I walked by an alley, grabbed my arm, and pulled me inside.

Zara stood beside her, both fully dressed in armor. "Where have you been?" she asked with a scowl.

"I'm sorry, girls, but I've got things to take care of," I said and stepped back from them.

"You go to fight the one who almost killed you," Zyra said. "We will accompany you."

I shook my head. "No. This is my fight. You need to stay as far away from me as you can. I only bring disaster to those who come near me."

"You need help," Zara said sternly. "He is too much for even you."

"I appreciate the sentiment, I really do, but you two go back to your father." I hugged them each, kissed their cheeks, and smiled sadly. "You two brought me a lot of joy over the years. I hope you know that."

"You speak as one who is set to kill herself," Zyra said and shook her head. "We will not allow it."

"I love you," I whispered, reared back, and sucker punched Zyra as hard as I could.

Zara caught her unconscious sister and I ran away as fast as I could, before they could come after me.

As I got closer, the scent of his power came to me, both repulsive and alluring simultaneously for me. One of the perks of being a tiger shark was the lateral line down my body that allowed me to pick up on changes in the water, but in my human form, it allowed me to pick up on changes in power. The scent led me to the bowling alley.

The bowling alley had shut down the same year that Bastian had attacked me. No one knew why it wasn't reopened, bulldozed, or changed. I had always sensed the darkness surrounding the building, and now that he was here, I knew why. This had always been a place for him. A place for his minions to gather information.

It made sense for him to have a base of operation in a city so close to the sea, a city so full of aquatic shifters. I should have burned the building down when I sensed the darkness, but I'd been trying to behave.

Atop the building were two winged figures. His minions.

They crowed loudly, announcing my arrival.

The double doors swung open, and soft music played inside.

Walking calmly inside the building, I prepared my mind and soul for the shitstorm I was about to endure. No matter what happened, I would free Theo.

No matter what happened, my life was worthless in comparison to hers. Her soul was pure and mine was dark.

She deserved to survive, to live a life of love and joy. To

find that which she had been unable to obtain because of society for so long.

I walked past the empty bowling lanes that flashed with a rainbow of colors, past the empty food court, past the bars ...

Pausing, I hopped over the bar top, grabbed a bottle of whiskey from the shelf, spun the cap off, and chugged it as I resumed my walk.

The music grew louder as I headed towards the back, down the stairs, down the long concrete hallway with creepily blinking lights, and to a set of metal double doors.

On the other side was magic so intense that my heart pounded in my ears and my skin crawled.

Definitely Bastian. He was definitely on the other side of those doors.

Taking an extra big drink, I wiped my mouth, kicked open the doors, and marched in like I owned the place.

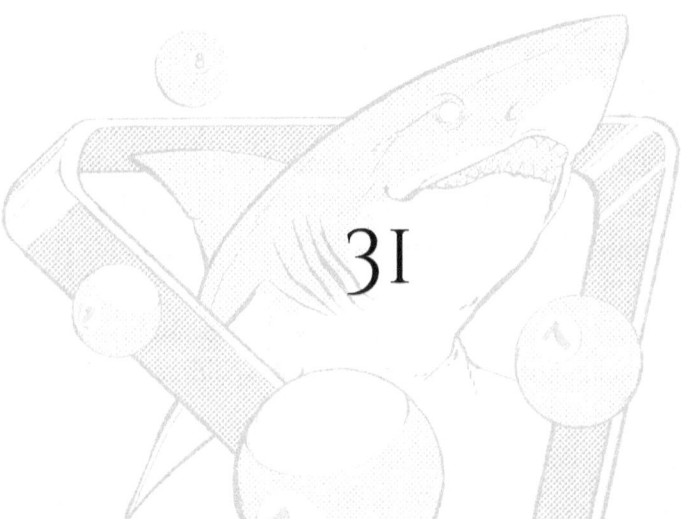

31

The room was large, rectangular, and mostly empty. Save for the four magical cages on either side of the walkway, and the throne with the man of my nightmares sitting upon it.

The four magical cages were teal in color, shaped like boxes, and housed one person in each.

My plan had been to barter for Theo, but my plans changed once I saw Silver sitting in the cage across from Theo. Bartering was no longer an option, which meant I had to prove I didn't care about them and send them on their way before Bastian did hurt them.

The other two in the cages were Bastian's minions, likely the ones who had tried to kill me.

Dammit. Damn Bastian! How had he found out about my love for Silver? There was no other reason for him to have the old codger.

Bastian lounged on his throne, his posture relaxed as he looked at me. "I was beginning to wonder if you would ever return," he said, his melodic voice causing a visceral reaction that almost had me gagging.

Instead of gagging, I chugged more whiskey. "I turned a bit feral," I admitted. "Why do you have an old man in a cage?"

Bastian's eyes flared gold a moment before he returned to his uncaring self. "There was a rumor that you had love for him. I worried I needed to kill him as competition for your love."

"You don't have to compete against anyone for my love," I said, not adding that it was because he would never fucking have it.

"Kass," Theo whispered.

I paused by her cage, turned my head, and looked down my nose at her. "Witch."

She flinched at first, but after staring into my eyes a moment longer, she finally realized I had to play this part to save her. "After all I've done for you, you're going to do me like that? You're just as bad as a man."

I shrugged, smirked, and said, "Survival is all that matters to me. You were a means to an end. Sorry, sugar."

"If I weren't in this cage, I would fuck you up," she snarled.

Tossing my head back, I laughed loudly. "You think you could hurt me? Please. I've faced and defeated *the* Sea Witch. You're nothing more than a peon."

"Have you unlocked it?" Bastian asked, bursting up to his feet.

"Unlocked what?" Silver asked.

I glanced at him, gave him a wink, and then took a step towards Bastian. "Why are they here? I thought this would be time for you and me to get reacquainted? Send them away.

Let them live their pathetic lives as a bartender and potion maker. We don't need them."

"You are better than this," Silver growled. "You are more than his minion. You do not want to be dominated by that trash."

To save him, I had to hurt him. I didn't want to do it, but I had to. I had to save him and I had to prove that I was powerful.

With a single punch, I shattered the cage around Silver, grabbed him by the collar, hauled him up to his feet, and snarled in his face. "Watch what you say, trash. If it weren't for all that I'd gotten from you, I would kill you right now." Silver was heavier than he looked, but I was able to toss him away from me, towards the exit. "Get out of here."

"You'll regret this, shark," Silver sneered.

I already did.

"Show me," Bastian said and reached out to grab my arm.

Despite the desire to pull away, I stayed still and let him wrap his hand around my arm and pull me closer to him. He stared down at me, searching my eyes, and then used his magic to search mine. Whatever he saw pleased him and he released me with a wide smile.

"Finally!" he shouted, his silver eyes even brighter than normal as he walked back to his throne and plopped down onto it. "Now, we will be unstoppable."

Silver left after one more look back at me.

He would be back, I knew that, but I needed to find a way to weaken Bastian before he returned, and I hoped he was going to bring back up.

Or, maybe I was wrong, and he was just going to abandon me like everyone else in my life. I didn't deserve them being in my life as it was, so I wouldn't put it past them abandoning me.

"What will we do with the witch?" I asked, chugging more of the whiskey.

"I kept her to try to get you to come," he admitted with a shrug. "It seems a swim in the depths has cleared your head and brought you back to me, how you should have been."

"Let's send her on her way and let her stew knowing she was nothing and is nothing," I suggested with a shrug.

"I don't know, we might be able to use her," he said softly.

I spun, glared at him, and asked, "Are you suggesting that I might have to share you?"

He straightened, stood, and walked up to me, his serious expression never wavering. "You will *never* have to share me."

"Yet, you have a woman in a cage before you," I snarled. "If you mean what you say, send her away so it is only us."

"We have enemies who are going to come and fight us," he said softly. "Her magic will be useful to us."

"So, you think she is more useful than me?" I snapped.

He bent down and whispered into my ear, "No one is more useful than you, my little shark. You are all that matters. Only you."

"Then send her away," I whisper-hissed.

He snapped his fingers and the cage around her disap-peared. She started to weave a spell, but I ran to her, wrapped her in a hug that looked like I was simply restraining her, and whispered, "Leave. Run. Don't look back. Flee. Now. Don't even think."

"No," she hissed.

"Tell them I'm sorry," I whispered. "Tell them this was the only way."

"Kass," she sobbed.

"You thought you could use a spell on us, but you're too slow. Beat it, you poor excuse for a potions' whore!" I yelled and stepped back from her.

With a deep breath, she smoothed down her clothes, gave me the most terrifying glare, and said, "I always thought you were just using me. I ignored everyone who even suggested it. You two deserve each other."

With a spin, she marched out and even though I knew what she had said was for show, it still stung.

"Now that we're alone, I want to discuss our future more with you," he said.

Shoving all of the emotions down into the box they belonged in, I turned, gave him a salacious smile, and sauntered up to his throne. "Do I get a fancy throne, too? Maybe a crown? I think I would look great in a crown."

He stood and waved me towards the throne. "I will defer my throne to you, and if you want a crown, I will get you one."

Without hesitation, I marched forward, slid onto the throne, and tossed a leg over the side. "So, you wanted to talk?"

He looked at me for a long, silent moment before nodding. "When we last met, you had magic within you that needed to be unlocked. A magic so powerful it will cripple him."

"Him?" I asked, sitting up a little straighter.

"Them," he said. "We will take the waters back and rule the seas like we are supposed to."

My hearing may not have been amazing, but there was zero chance that I had misheard him. So, this wasn't just a trip down power lane, but revenge lane.

Interesting.

"Ruling the seas sounds nice," I admitted. "Those fucking orcas and dolphins have always pissed me off."

The more honest I was with him, the lower the chances of him catching wind that I didn't really give a crap about his desire for dominance. Sure, I would love to beat the blowholes off the dolphins and orcas, but I didn't want to kill all of them. I didn't want to commit genocide.

"What's our first step?" I asked, and started bouncing my leg. "Do you have some new powers? Some amazing plan with lots of steps and details? Some group of amazing new minions I've yet to meet?"

He scowled and although I wasn't certain how, it was obvious I had hit a nerve. "First, we're going to take back Atlantis."

My eyes nearly popped out of my head. "Atlantis? You know where it is?" In a decade, no one had found the lost city, and not for lack of trying. Even I had ventured out a few times after hearing some tidbits I thought were related.

He nodded. "I just need you by my side to take it back. We're going to leave tomorrow morning."

My brows furrowed. Why did he need me? He was much stronger than me.

"What do we do in the meantime?" I asked.

"I need to gather some resources and speak to my minions, the ones that remain," he said, and pulled out a cellphone.

I stood and dusted my pants off. "Well, then I'll go grab my things and meet you at the pier in the morning."

He scowled and stepped in front of me, blocking my path out of the room. "You stay with me."

My brow arched. "Really? You don't trust me? I didn't have to come back. I could have stayed in the ocean and remained a shark. For our relationship to work, you need to trust me."

After what felt like an eternity, he nodded. "You're right. Meet me at the pier at nine o'clock."

With a hop, I got to my feet, kissed his cheek, and chugged the whiskey to wipe away his taste from my lips as I walked calmly out of the room.

Asking him to let me leave had been a gamble. Truthfully, I thought he wouldn't buy my act at all, since the last time I'd seen him, I had bitten his arm off. Did that say something about how much he needed me? Why did he need me? What was he going to gain by having me by his side, that he only realized after I had left?

I knew that even though he'd given in and let me go, I needed to continue playing this part, because he would no doubt have people follow me and keep tabs on me.

No matter how badly I wanted to speak to my friends, I couldn't. Theo would understand, as would Silver. I just hoped the others would, too.

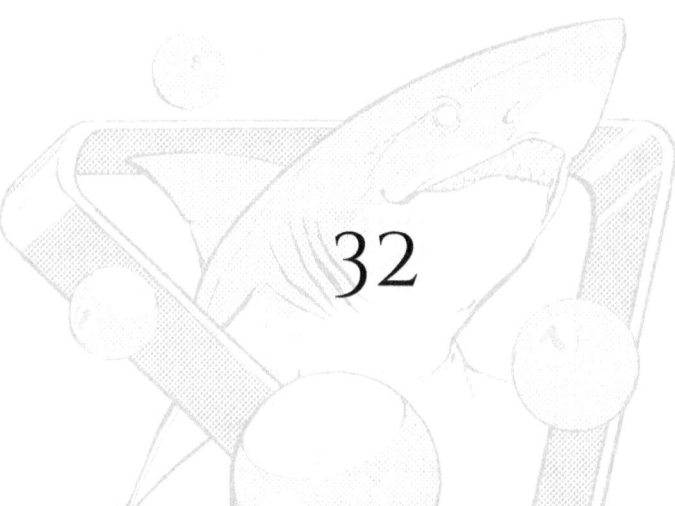

32

Instead of immediately leaving the alley, I sat at the bar within the alley, drinking more of my bottle, and tried to figure out how my life had turned out this way.

When I was a child, my parents had spent most of our time together in shark form. My father, whose face was nothing, but a shadow, had taught me how to switch to my human form, and keep my gills at the same time, so I could be in or out of the water without breathing issues. My mother had spent most of our time teaching me to protect myself while in shark form.

They'd abandoned me to the ocean sometime shortly after my tenth birthday, and no matter how far I swam, how many creatures I asked, they were nowhere to be found. Honestly, I really just wanted to know what had become of them.

Were they murdered? Died of old age? Abandoned me because I was too much? Abandoned me to protect me from some crazy, power-hungry person?

Okay, the last one was a total stretch, but you have a lot of free time to come up with ideas while you're swimming through the ocean.

Tilting the bottle back, I was disheartened to find it as empty as my heart. With a sigh, I tossed the bottle, hopped over the bar top, and grabbed another one.

Holding the bottle against my cheek, I smiled and purred. "Hello, beautiful. You and I are going to be friends for the rest of your life. Though, your life may only be an hour or two if your previous companion is anything to go by."

The bottle did not laugh at my funny joke, so I unscrewed its cap and chugged several large gulps of its innards instead.

I finished that bottle and another before deciding it was time to leave. Grabbing the last bottle on the shelf, not even sure what type of alcohol it was, and not caring, I swiped the back of my hand across my mouth, and walked out of the alley and out into the noisy night.

People walked, talked, and laughed together like any other night. Like the world wasn't close to ending and I wasn't going to likely lose my soul and life soon. Like I hadn't just lost what was likely my one chance at love.

Stumbling, I chugged the alcohol and pushed through the obnoxiously joyous people.

Some yelled at me, some cursed at me, and some spat insults at me.

I didn't give a shit what they thought. They could all rot in Davy Jones's locker.

Although, I knew I didn't really feel that way, since part of why I was giving in to Bastian was to prevent him from hurting the innocents in this city. There were so many in the world who could not protect themselves.

A dark figure stepped out of the alley to my left, but I sidestepped their attempted punch. My feet tangled and I landed hard on my butt.

"Ouch," I hissed, glad I was able to save my bottle from hitting the ground with my quick reflexes.

The dark figure was much blurrier than it should have been and suddenly split into several of them.

"P-piss off," I slurred as I staggered to a stand, clutching my bottle tightly between my breasts, so it didn't spill. "It's my last night of freedom, and I want to enjoy it."

"The fuck she just say?" a somewhat familiar male voice asked.

With a glare, that was really hard to hold since my eyes couldn't focus, I turned and continued down the sidewalk and took another chug out of the bottle.

This time, I wasn't prepared for the dark, blurry figures and they managed to grab my hands and force them behind my back.

"Don't spill my booze!" I shouted as I struggled. If they broke my bottle, I would cut their hands off.

A bag was shoved over my head, but it thankfully didn't smell. Last time I'd been kidnapped, the bag had smelled like week-old fish and it had taken ten showers to get it out of my hair.

"You really should learn how to kidnap someone. At least like a dozen people saw you just now. I don't know what you look like, but I'm sure they do. That was stupid. Also, you should have gagged me. I'm not going to shut up. You'll want to kill me before you sell me or whatever it is you think you're going to do. Honestly, you should just let me go. There's a powerful and scary man after me, and if you don't let me go, he's going to kill you."

They didn't talk, just forced me to walk, and took me down streets with people talking and laughing without a care in the world. None tried to help me, but I should have expected that.

My kidnappers didn't speak, but that was fine. Once we got wherever they were taking me and removed the bag, I would beat the crap out of them.

One great thing about my genetics and magic was that I sobered up relatively quickly.

Doors opened and shut, the cool night breeze disappeared, and the ground grew softer, likely carpet.

So, we were indoors now.

Magic flared around me, making the hair on the back of my neck stand on end.

Ropes were tied around my wrists, securing me to the chair they made me sit on. The bag was removed and I was grateful that the lights were dimmed so my eyes immediately adjusted.

Grant, Reed, Jong-hyun, and Jong-min stood in front of me.

"You fucking idiots," I hissed, and pulled against the restraints on my arms. "Let me go right now. He's going to kill you if he finds out you kidnapped me."

"Why did you go to him?" Grant asked. His eyes were glowing and to most he might have looked angry, but I could see deep within that I had hurt him.

"He had Theo and Silver captive," I answered. "Those two took me in when no one else would, and became my family. I will sacrifice myself a thousand times to protect them."

"He wants to use you," Jong-min said.

I nodded. "I know."

"You have a plan?" Reed asked.

I shrugged one shoulder. "Maybe."

"You're going to get yourself killed," Jong-min snapped.

"Most likely," I agreed.

"No," Reed said, his voice deep and his eyes golden.

"Handsome, you don't get to decide what I do with my body," I said with a smile, trying to lighten the mood.

"You're going to let him use you, discard you, and then he's going to come back here and hurt everyone anyways," Grant said.

"No, he's going to die," I said. "And you morons will, too, if you don't let me go. I don't need you to rescue me. I'm a big girl, and I'm making this decision of my own free will."

"No, you're not," Silver said from my right.

My head whipped to the side so fast that I got the spins. I closed my eyes and moaned. "Spins. Spins. Yuck. Oh, chum."

"How much did she drink?" Silver asked as he squatted down beside me.

"Four-ish bottles," I whispered.

He cursed in his native language. "You trying to kill yourself early?"

"What's it matter, when I'm going to die in a few days anyway?" I asked. "My liver just needs to function for a few more days."

"Child, he isn't as strong as you think," Silver whispered.

I opened my eyes and stared into his as I whispered, "He got you."

Silver snarled. "Yeah, he tricked me and got me. He also talked a lot in front of me. The only way he can succeed with his plan is with you at his side."

"I have to go with him," I said sternly. "He knows where my home is."

"Your home?" All five men asked simultaneously.

33

I nodded. "It's been so long, and I haven't been able to find it, but he claims that he's found it. My parents could be there. I might find more of my people."

"We are your people." Silver growled and stood. "We may not be flesh and blood related, but you are my family and I love you as much as my other daughters."

Tears formed in my eyes and I sniffled a little. Why did this old man have to say such things when I was about to sacrifice myself?

"Where is your home?" Reed asked.

"Deep in the ocean," I answered. "So, none of you can come. Please, let me go. I must leave with him tomorrow morning. If you try to hold me against my will, I will do whatever I must to escape. Even harm you ... or myself."

Five deep growls reverberated around me.

"How do you deal with this?" Jong-min asked Silver.

Silver ran a hand down his face. "She's always been a damn handful, but this is not a side of her I have experienced before. Kass, you have friends now. We can gather our resources and—"

While they'd been talking, I had slowly changed the skin on my wrists to my shark skin. With a sharp tug, I snapped the ropes and stood. "I am sorry for the pain and frustration I have caused you all." Facing the five of them, I bent at the waist and bowed to them. "I am very sorry." Straightening, I walked up to Silver and jumped up to kiss his cheek. "Thank you for taking care of this little girl, and being the father figure I had always wanted."

"Don't do this, child. I've fought many battles, and I'm not done yet. Let me fight at your side," he whispered, tears glazing over his eyes.

"Not this time, Father."

He turned away, his hands clenched into fists as he looked out the large window of what I realized was the guys' hotel room.

I spun and faced the foursome. "I think we could have been great together, but unfortunately, fate has other ideas for me. I'm pretty sure she brought you to me just to taunt me with what could have been. Thank you for spending time with me and befriending me. I hope you know that my time with you was one of my favorite times on land." Looking specifically at Grant and Reed, I smiled and said, "You two will always hold a special place in my heart. Thank you."

Grant stepped forward, scooped me up, and kissed me deeply. Once done devouring my mouth, and leaving me lightheaded, he whispered, "Please, don't go. Let us show you what more could come of us."

Reed took me from Grant, and it was surprising how much I enjoyed being held against their chests in such an intimate manner. Reed kissed my forehead and whispered, "I understand that you need to go. I do. Can you please try to come back? Please. Please kill that bastard, and then do everything in your power to return to us. I know it may not be this week or month, but even if it's a year from now, please come back and find us."

"I don't want to die," I whispered, and wrapped my arms around his neck. "My goal is to kill him and free the ocean of his taint. If I can come back, I will, but please don't wait for me. Don't waste what is left of your life waiting for me. I don't know if I can get a message to you if I do die."

"We'll know," he whispered and nuzzled behind my ear. "If you die, we will know. I will know."

"What?" I asked, but he set me down and turned away without answering.

Jong-min held out a leather-wrapped item. "This will help you."

I took it and smiled wide. "Thank you, Jong-min."

He never dropped his stoic expression, but it softened a little as he said, "You may call me Min."

My eyes widened and my mouth would have dropped if I hadn't clamped it shut and bowed to him. "Thank you, Min."

Jong-hyun stepped forward and hugged me. With his hand on my back, a jolt of energy pierced my back and he whispered, "Stay safe. You may call me Hyun."

I squeezed him and whispered, "Thank you, Hyun."

With the goodbyes out of the way, I walked to the door, but stopped with my hand hovering above the handle. Why was this goodbye so hard? I barely knew them.

"Tell Theo I love her, please?"

"I will," Silver promised.

"Tell your daughters I am sorry, too. They made my life so much better, and I loved them like sisters," I whispered, and felt the tears stinging my eyes.

"I will tell them," Silver promised again.

With a nod, I jerked open the door and rushed out. The tears began to spill, so I ran down the stairs, out of the hotel, and to an empty alley, where I could cry without an audience.

This cry was definitely my ugliest one, but I didn't care, since there was no one to see me. My heart hurt so much, that I clutched my chest and wished I could tear it out to make it stop.

Opening the leather-wrapped object from Jong-min, my tears and sobs were even harder as I stared down at the black and white cat's paw. It was a magic talisman, an item that stored magical power that could be used in an emergency when the wearer had run out of magic.

I had said I would try to survive, and I would, but I had very little hope that I could.

Wrapping my arms around myself, I sat against the brick building as I continued to cry, and for a moment dreamed of what life might be like if I did return. Maybe, just maybe, I could defeat Bastian without dying. Then, I could return and sweep those four men off their feet and start a glorious relationship.

If Theo didn't kill me when I returned first.

That thought had me chuckling, and it wasn't long before I finally fell asleep.

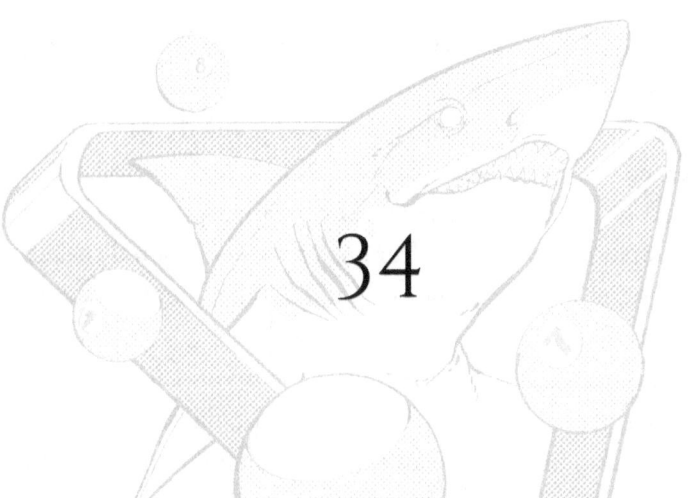

34

My back was sore from sleeping in the alley, which added to my grumpiness as I shuffled to the pier.

"You showed," Bastian said with wide eyes.

Four of his minions stood behind him, their heads down, but I could see them looking at me. Three of them were dolphin shifters, but the fourth one was a pale girl who was glaring daggers at me. She might be a problem I would have to deal with before Bastian. Judging by the glare she was giving me, she didn't like that I was taking Bastian's attention.

Did she think I was a love rival?

Ew.

I arched a brow at Bastian. "I told you I would."

He cleared his throat and nodded. "Well, let's be on our way."

Normally, I would have waited for him, but knowing he wasn't going to kill me, I just leaped over the railing and down into the water first. He could have my back all he wanted.

As soon as my fingertips touched the water, I shifted into

my full shark form and swam in a circle to wait for Bastian, since I didn't know the way.

He dove in, still in human form and pointed east.

Once we were out deeper, he switched forms, and I couldn't lie and say it didn't take my breath away.

Bastian was a kraken, after all, a very endangered species with a lot of magic and power. And so many tentacles ... so many.

For days we swam, eating fish his minions caught for us, until we finally made it to a break point at Dila Island.

Dila Island used to be an oasis for human pirates, but the aquatic shifters took it over a few decades ago for a safe haven. The human pirates had cut down a lot of the flora to build houses and buildings, but those were gone now and the flora was once again flourishing.

With a sigh, I lay on the beach and stared up at the stars overhead.

What was Theo doing right now? Was she at Silver's? Was she pissed at me, or was she glad to be rid of my baggage? To be rid of me?

Had the foursome found a new woman to spread her legs for them? It wouldn't be hard.

Well, they would be.

Dammit. I missed them so much.

Silver was likely serving drinks, just like he had before I'd stumbled into his bar. He would forget about me in time and continue on with his life, likely better for it.

Without me there, there would be fewer fights, and the patrons would have more money to spend on drinks, since I wouldn't be taking it from them by swindling them at pool.

I enjoyed being a pool shark. I enjoyed the pun that I had become. That life had been nice, cushy, and warm.

"What has your brows drawn so?" Bastian asked as he sat beside me.

"Why do you need me to get into Atlantis?" I asked. "Is there a magical barrier, or something?"

"Something like that," he answered vaguely and looked out across the water.

"You tried to kill me before. What makes you so sure that you need me now?" I asked. "What if I can't help you get into Atlantis? Will you kill me?" There was no fear in my voice, as I didn't fear my death. Not any longer. Sure, I didn't want to die, but death was inevitable, and I had had some great years on land with my friends. I only regretted not finding love.

"I was defeated as soon as I hurt you. I truly believe if I hadn't made that bond with you, that I would have been killed. How did you remove the bond, anyway? I hid it within your mind where you wouldn't notice it."

So that was the darkness in my head that the twins had cured.

"A spell to cure darkness," I admitted. "A vampire had marked me and I wanted his mark gone. I didn't realize your mark was there until I got rid of his as well."

Bastian scowled. "My bond is not dark like a vampire's."

Scoffing would give away how I really felt about him, so I bit my tongue and watched the stars twinkle overhead instead.

"You were young, and I regret harming you. My goal was simply to set order to the oceans, like there should be. There are so many weaklings allowed to rule, while forcing the truly powerful cower in the dark. I cannot let that stand. I need to set the balance as it should be."

Why did the big bad guy always think they had great reasons and were doing things that were for the betterment of everyone else? He was a power-hungry, revenge-starved asshole, and that's all there was to it. He wanted to kill us all, not make a better place for us.

I would still let him monologue and hope he gave away more of his plan, though.

"There are many who hurt others," I agreed with a nod. The girl who was in love with him was making her way across the sand towards us. "There are many dolphins and orcas who tried to kill me over the years. In fact, that minion female over there clearly hates me."

He glanced at the girl and then looked back at me. "Are you jealous?"

Was it possible for your eyebrows to shoot off your head from shock?

"Of course not. Why would you even ask that? She's been glaring at me and clearly plotting my demise since she saw me."

"She's harmless," he said, and waved his hand dismissively. "She is a good minion and does as she is asked, though. She's been with me for about five years now."

"Hm," I said, letting him know I wasn't buying it.

"Her loyalty is unwavering," he said with certainty.

"Well, I'm glad you found someone like that to stay at your side," I said and was shocked that the words sounded genuine. Damn, I was turning into an even better liar than before. That was pretty impressive, if I did say so myself.

"I've been searching for you for so long, that I feel like I'm dreaming now that I finally have you at my side," he said. "I was worried when I saw you with those land bastards, but clearly, you knew they weren't good enough for you."

Had I been a growling type, I would have growled. Did he really think he was better than the foursome? No. He was trash when compared to them. I would choose the foursome over him in whatever life we had. They were snarky bastards, but they were honest and not out to boil the seas.

"How did you find out about Theo?" I asked.

He scoffed. "Everyone knew that you two were friends. Everyone I talked to always discussed you two being together, and how close you were. I almost killed her just for how close you were, but thought it might upset you if I killed her without talking to you first."

"Yes, I would have been irritated, but only because I wouldn't have had a chance to tell her to her face that I had just been using her. Now, she knows that she was nothing more than a tool for me to use. Just like everyone else in that town," I said sternly. Had he killed Theo, I would have obliterated him and spread his pieces all across the ocean. Or maybe I would have just barbecued him and eaten him. That would have been much more fun.

He didn't respond, so I asked another question to keep him talking.

"What enabled you to finally find Atlantis?"

He sighed and shook his head. "It took me this entire time to locate it. I created a map of the seas and searched each quadrant very carefully. When I finally did find it, I was in disbelief and searched a few other quadrants before returning to that one to confirm."

"What's keeping you from entering?" I asked.

"A barrier of some kind," he muttered, while looking out at the sea and narrowing his eyes.

"And you think I'll be able to get through the barrier?"

He nodded, but just continued staring at the sea.

Well, since I wouldn't get anything else out of him, it was a good time to rest and take a nap. I had to stay sharp and prepared to protect myself from whatever they were going to throw at me.

Part of me was worried I wouldn't be allowed to make it through the barrier Bastian spoke about. What if I wasn't worthy or it wouldn't let me through? Sure, I was born there, but it had been a long time since I set fin inside.

What were my friends doing right now? Was Theo angry at me, or did she understand?

Did Silver explain everything to the girls, or would they be out for my head if I returned?

When I returned. I was going to return to at least apologize to them properly once this was all over.

"Time to go," the female who hated me said in a smooth voice.

I cracked open one eye. She was only a foot away from me, and her eyes glowed with an eerie magic.

I showed her my teeth. "Thanks for the heads up."

When she didn't leave immediately, I let my smile spread to show her more of my teeth. She swallowed, took the hint, and scurried across the sand to Bastian's side.

Yep, she was going to be trouble.

35

Deciding my life wasn't dangerous enough already, I walked over, getting as close to Bastian's side as I could without touching him, and batted my eyelashes. "Are we ready to go?"

If looks could kill, I'd be a seagull buffet right now.

Bastian smiled down at me and nodded. "Yes. Glad to see you're warming up to fate."

Fate was bullshit, and I would never be his, but I would play along.

I shrugged, put my arms behind my back, and said, "Why fight it, right?"

"Let's get back into the sea and finish our journey," he said, beaming like a kid in a candy store.

"We'll arrive within the day?" I asked, both excited and terrified at the same time.

He nodded. "Yes."

Without waiting for him, I dove into the sea and shifted as soon as the cold ocean water touched me. I wouldn't admit it to him, but I could feel a pull on my soul, my very center, towards what I hoped was home. To not give that away, I swam in the direction we'd started, and then waited for him to lead.

The girl, whose name I should really learn, made sure to quickly get to his side and block the spot from me.

She shouldn't have done that. Now, I was totally going to make a point of getting in her way and harassing her.

For now, I let her swim beside him. She was a seal shifter with a gorgeous spotted coat.

Would it be possible to let her live, or would I have to kill her before this was all over?

The fact that I didn't really care either way really said something about my life.

As we swam, I kept an eye on his minions, who had basically surrounded me. Even though Bastian claimed he wanted to keep me alive, that didn't mean an overzealous minion wouldn't try to kill me.

And, I didn't fully trust Bastian. He was crazy, and I had to keep on my guard to stay safe.

Almost the entire day was spent swimming, thankfully at a slow pace that wouldn't tax my body. The last thing I needed was to be exhausted when we made it to Atlantis.

I swam in a circle and wondered what the aquarium would tell the visitors about me? Would that little girl come back to see me and be sad I was missing? Would they tell her I was dead or just say I was sick? If anything, I hoped they told them I was released into the wild.

That damn turtle would likely sleep a lot better now that I wasn't in the tank with him. Dumb turtle.

A deep pulse of magic hit me in the chest and made my entire body tense in pain before relaxing again.

Bastian increased his speed, and it took me a second to catch up as the magic lingered within my fins.

When I finally caught up to him, he had stopped and was staring intently at a dark cloud ahead.

The dark cloud was abnormal, like a storm cloud, but deep in the depths of the ocean.

He looked at me and bobbed his head once.

Okay, so that must be the boundary that kept him away. It looked terrifying, and I worried what might be lurking beneath the darkness.

With a twitch of my tail, I pushed forward, closed my eyes, and prayed to be let through.

Meeting no resistance, I cracked open an eye and nearly shifted in surprise at the sight of my home before me.

Atlantis looked exactly as I remembered it, an underwater city with lots of golden decorations, and teeming with aquatic life.

Two great white sharks swam towards me, spun around me once, and then shifted into human forms.

"Sister, you have been gone a long time," the one on the left said.

Sister?

Wait, he'd said that in my mind! Telepathy!

"Y-you know me?" I asked back.

"We recognize our own," the one on the right answered.

"Come, let us take you to the leaders," the one on the left said.

They both shifted, so I followed suit. Part of me was nervous to follow these strangers, but I didn't sense any malice from them.

They swam in front of me, completely giving me their

tails, which made me trust them more, but also made me concerned their egos were large. Who gave a random person their back so freely? Unless they truly did recognize that I was from here and trusted me not to attack one of our own.

Still a stupid idea to give someone your back when you didn't know them.

The underwater city had so many different aquatic species, all of whom were watching me with interest.

The buildings were in perfect condition, with tall spires, and strange symbols I did not recognize.

The largest building had a circular dome at the top with several hippocampus statues around the edge of the dome, like gargoyles on a cathedral.

A large opening at the front of the building allowed us to swim inside unfettered.

Inside, the ceilings were covered in paintings of a man with a coral crown on a chariot pulled by two hippocampi, with an army of aquatic creatures behind him, facing off against a man wearing a thorn crown on a chariot pulled by tigers with an army of land creatures behind him.

Deep within the building was a horseshoe-shaped stage with three men and two women seated in their human forms. Why were they seated like that? Did they know I was coming? Or did they always sit there? Why weren't they in animal form either?

This entire set up didn't make sense and it was bothering me.

For a moment, the entire building and all of the people flickered, like lag on a screen.

I stopped swimming and blinked a few times.

Everything looked normal again.

Had I imagined it? I must have. Too much time swimming and being paranoid with Bastian and his minions around me.

"Why have you returned?" the woman in the center demanded.

All five stood from their chairs and changed their skin so that scales covered them.

I paused, still not used to speaking telepathically, shifted, and asked, "What do you mean?"

"You and your family were banished!" the man to her left shouted, his teeth elongated as soon as he finished. Definitely a shark, too.

Banished? What? Why would my parents have been banished? They never mentioned it to me.

"I was a child when I left and my parents disappeared when I was only ten years old. I have no memory of what you're saying," I replied calmly.

They were pretty worked up about me being back and were acting really strange. Almost like ... they were scared of me.

"Guards, move away from her," the woman in the center ordered.

The two guards swam away from me, turning to face me instead, ready to fight.

"I don't understand. Why are you treating me like an enemy?" My words came out soft and my heart constricted.

I hadn't expected a party to be thrown in my honor when I returned, but hostility was definitely not what I had anticipated. Why did they hate me so much?

The leaders looked at each other, brows furrowed.

Finally, after a long silence, the woman in the center, who

by now seemed like their spokesperson, explained. "You have a power that is catastrophic when used around those of Atlantis. Your power is one passed down due to a perverse relationship in your lineage between an Atlantean and a land dweller."

I scoffed and shook my head. "I don't have any powers. I'm an average shark shifter. I'm actually one of the smallest tiger shark shifters I've ever seen."

The leaders rippled a moment, like a wave had made their entire bodies distort.

What was going on? Something was very, very wrong. This entire interaction was wrong. My vision was messed up or something.

"You must remember," the woman growled. "You must remember what you did that caused your parents to take you and leave Atlantis."

"I don't remember shit!" I shouted. "So, just tell me!"

"Remember!" one of the guards shouted.

My head throbbed painfully, and I clutched it tightly. "What are you doing?" I gasped.

"Remember!" they all shouted simultaneously, increasing the pain tenfold.

36

Their images wavered again, and then the memory hit me like a brick to the face. Yes, I did know what that felt like, thanks to a drunken argument with a human man whose money I'd won from a dozen pool matches.

My parents had been tiger shark shifters, too. My mother had lots of stripes, her body a glorious coloring in shark form, and some of her stripes carried over to her human form as well. My father was incredibly large in both shark and human form, and I had loved to be carried by him. I had felt so safe in his arms.

While playing with some other children, an octopus shifter, a squid shifter, and two shark shifters, they'd accidentally hurt me. When I'd cried out in pain, they had also cried out in pain and reverted to their human forms. Everyone around us had reverted to their human forms as well.

Mom and Dad had rushed to me. Dad gathered me up in his arms and consoled me. When I'd stopped crying, guards had forced us to gather our things and leave Atlantis. The leaders had stood at the exit and I remembered the woman in the center. Ashta was her name. She'd stared at me in horror and said, "She has the power to steal our shifting. The stones power her, and we cannot allow her to be here. We cannot allow her to stay and make us weak."

"She could learn to control it," Dad said adamantly. "Now that we know she has this ability, we can teach her."

Ashta shook her head. "She must leave, and never return."

"I'm not sending my child out into the open ocean alone," Mom snarled. "She will not survive being so young and never hunting by herself yet."

"We will go with her," Dad said sternly as he continued to cradle me.

"She may never return here," Ashta ordered. "You may return, but she cannot."

Mom and Dad nodded.

"We understand," Dad said, kissed the top of my head, and swam out into the ocean.

The memory dissipated, my headache disappeared, and when I opened my eyes again, Atlantis was gone as well.

Bastian stared at me with a huge smile, wide eyes, and a gleam in his eyes that I did not like.

"Wh-what happened?" I asked as I looked around. My arms felt heavy and when I tried to move them, realized that they were tied with chains behind my back. I struggled against the chains, but they burned against my skin when I did. "What's going on?" We floated deep beneath the ocean's surface in the middle of nowhere. "Where's Atlantis? Where are the leaders? Why am I chained?"

"All of your questions will be answered soon," Bastian said. He swam closer to me, dragged a finger down my cheek and whispered, "I knew you were the answer. I knew it was you who would help me defeat him."

I tried to shift, but felt too weak and tired. Were the chains spelled?

"Let me go!" I ordered him with a snarl.

He swam closer, lining his body up with mine, so that we touched from forehead to toes, bent so his mouth was beside my ear, and whispered, "Never."

Before I could tear his throat out, he swam back, waved at someone behind me, and swam off into the waters.

"What the fuck is going on?" I shouted. My shout caused ripples in the water and Bastian stopped swimming.

He turned and said, "We haven't made it to Atlantis yet. I stopped us early, so that my minions could use their powers to make you hallucinate and think you were there. We needed to know what your power was, so that we would know how to use it once we arrived at Atlantis. They helped you unlock those memories you were too young to recall yourself easily. Now we know just how powerful and amazing you truly are. Now we know that together, we can take back your rightful homeland from those who sent you away."

"I'm not going to help you take over Atlantis." He was absolutely delusional if he thought I would help him. Even if they had sent me away, I wasn't out to get revenge against them.

"Darling, you don't have a choice," he said with a wink, and swam off again.

The seal girl swam out from behind me, a chain in her hands and said, "I'll drag you all the way if I have to. Just follow along nicely."

Giving her my widest smile, I said, "It's been a long time since I've eaten seal. Before this trip is over, I'm going to roast your flesh and devour every inch of you, including your soul."

Her face paled, but she turned and started swimming, dragging me on the chain behind her. Being the petty bitch I was, I let her drag me and didn't even bother trying to swim or kick my legs. My arms were bound tightly in the chains, so there was no way I could shift or swim that way. I could have shifted my legs into a tail, but I still felt lethargic.

If they could make me hallucinate, then that meant I couldn't trust anything that I saw. That meant I had to be very careful with my reactions to things. Knowing they could do it, made the way the people had kept looking distorted make sense. They weren't real, and my brain had been trying to show me that it was fake. Had tried to warn me that things were not as they seemed.

How could I react, if I had no idea if what I was seeing was real? I couldn't kill without worrying it was someone else. I couldn't help someone without worrying it was actually an enemy.

If the Chums or any of the friends I had showed up, I would have to assume they were fake and Bastian was testing my loyalty.

For the first time in a decade, I felt truly and utterly helpless.

I missed Theo.

37

Citizens of Atlantis swam away in fear, women, men, and children fleeing as quickly as they could from the intruders.

I wanted to break free, protect them, tell them I wasn't with these psychopaths, but I couldn't do anything.

I was worthless. Weak. Pathetic.

At the entrance to the circular building, Bastian paused and turned to face me.

"Now is when you prove your loyalty to me."

I bobbed my head. "I can do that. I'm so loyal. Super loyal."

Seal girl rolled her eyes and turned away from me.

"If you try to betray me—"

Without letting him finish, I said, "Right, you'll kill me and strip the meat from my bones. Understood."

He snapped his fingers and the chains fell away.

I saluted him. "Ready when you are."

After a long stare down, he swam into the building.

Pretty certain that was my cue to follow, I swam inside.

The people I had seen in the vision earlier were seated

like they had shown me, but their faces had a few more wrinkles and their hair sported a few more gray hairs.

"What are you doing here? What is *she* doing here?" one of the older men yelled as he swam up over his seat.

"Yes, well, I've come to kill you all and take over Atlantis," Bastian said with a smile.

This was it. This was where I had to make my move. Logic told me I would fail and die, but there wasn't anything else I could do. I couldn't let him take over my home. To become even *more* powerful. He needed to die.

Seal girl and the others swam inside, fanning out around the back of the room.

The other elders took in the scene calmly, and I hoped they had some hidden powers up their sleeves.

"You have three seconds to leave," the woman in the middle ordered. "Otherwise, we will obliterate you."

"I'm here against my will!" I shouted. "I didn't want to come here."

She looked at me, her eyes widened, started glowing, and she shouted, "Get out of here!"

This was my chance.

I jerked back and grunted. "She's ... she's compelling me to leave!" I shouted, my voice sounded scared and frantic as I'd intended.

The woman's brows furrowed a moment, but then she yelled so loud that the walls shook. "Leave!"

With an arch of my back, I propelled myself farther back out of the building. It wasn't much, but if I could leave, could ensure they could shift, I might be able to save them.

Or at least give them a fighting chance.

Once I was outside of the building, I exhaled in relief.

The fighting inside was loud, bright, and small streams of blood seeped out on the currents. There was so much, I knew a few of the elders weren't going to survive.

What more could I do besides leave? Besides give them the ability to shift?

So useless!

No, I wasn't useless. I could do something. I could help. I just had to figure out how.

"What are you doing?" one of Bastian's minions asked as he swam outside. He was a stingray shifter, which meant he likely used assassination tactics to kill his enemies and wasn't great at head-to-head combat.

"She forced me outside," I said. "Her magic was too strong to fight."

He scowled. "Have you tried coming back in?"

"I didn't want to interrupt Bastian," I said, and looked down bashfully.

Fall for it. Fall for it!

He swam closer, finally within range. "He's worried about you not being in there."

"He should be worried about sending you out here alone," I said, shifted, and bit his upper body.

He yelled, and tried to hit my nose, but I shook him as hard as I could, my teeth tearing through skin, muscle, and bone easily. Half of his body tore off and blood filled the area. Not wasting my time, I clamped my jaws over his head, right at his neck, shook my head twice, and tore his head from his body. I had to make sure he was dead and couldn't report back to Bastian.

One minion down.

I peeked inside and thanked whatever god was listening for his help as the other minion was right by the door.

Bastian was fighting two of the elders and seal girl was completely focused on their battle.

Quickly, I swam inside, latched onto the minion – this one was a giant squid – and dragged him out of the room to kill him.

He tried to shift, but I killed him before he could.

Seal girl came out, saw the two bodies, and started whispering a spell. I spun around and smacked her with my tail before she could finish, her body hit the wall of the building and she grunted.

"I knew you weren't loyal. That you would try to betray him," she snarled.

Since I was fully shifted, I couldn't respond verbally, so I opted for physically responding. I charged forward and tried to clamp my jaws around her head, but she shifted into her seal form and darted away.

Seals were fast and nimble, but they were always cocky, and I knew without a doubt she was one of the cockiest seals I had ever met. That meant I'd be able to kill her quick.

I pulled my lips up to show her my teeth and gave chase, trying to make her get stuck on the buildings, but she sensed my moves and swam higher, into the open sea.

That was her first mistake. In the open sea, I could swim faster.

For what felt like hours, I chased her, my teeth grazing her tail a few times, but she was too quick and escaped each time.

Unfortunately for her, she required oxygen. I let her go to

the surface without chase twice to lull her into a sense of security.

The third time, I swam as fast as I could, launched myself up and out of the water, her body in my mouth.

A boat full of humans with cameras was nearby, and their cameras flashed like crazy as I flew up into the air. Giving them an extra show, and to end this quickly, I bit her in half before falling back into the water.

Her upper half still swam weakly, and I finished her off quickly.

Sinking slowly back down towards the city, I let my body recover some of its endurance. She'd put up quite a fight, but her cockiness had ended up being her downfall.

As I neared the building again, I steeled myself for this fight. I wasn't the same girl I had been last time we faced off.

This time, I would beat him.

A dark shadow passed over me and I immediately spun around to look up.

My entire body froze as I watched the giant, tentacled head lean down to look into the building.

"Worry not, child. I am not here for you," his deep voice said in my head.

"He ... he really was insane and thought he was going to be able to fight you, wasn't he?" I asked. I had considered this was who he had meant when he said I could help him defeat "him," but hadn't thought he was that stupid.

Wait, was this another hallucination? Was this something Bastian was making me see? Or was Cthulhu really here? No, I'd killed the seal. This had to be real. Cthulhu was really here right now, and I was incredibly unsure how to feel about that. Okay, I did know how I felt: terrified. Incredibly terrified that I was about to die at the hands of an elder being.

The deep chuckle shook the entire ocean. *"Yes, but have no fear, I will destroy him soon enough, and I know that you are here against your will."*

I bowed my head and swam slowly in a circle to watch Bastian's downfall, while trying to remain sane at having just talked to Cthulhu. Keeping my head bowed allowed me to look at them, but not directly at Cthulhu, I knew better than to meet his gaze.

Cthulhu reached forward with a webbed hand, grabbed the top of the building, squeezed, and ripped the ceiling off. *"There, much easier to see you little worms now,"* he said.

"You won't defeat me!" Bastian yelled.

I blinked slowly. Had ... had he really just talked back to Cthulhu?

"I indulged you far too long. It's time I rid the world of you," Cthulhu said with a long sigh.

Bastian swam up out of the building, shifted into his kraken form, and grabbed me in one of his tentacles.

I thrashed about, tried to break free, tried to bite him, but couldn't reach him. He instantly began to steal my magic from me.

How? How was he taking my magic?

Cthulhu sighed, grabbed Bastian and mentally ordered, *"Release the shark right now."*

Bastian released me, but the damage was already done, my magic already stolen. I drifted to the sea floor, and watched as Bastian tried to use magic against one of the oldest beings in the universe. He tried to force Cthulhu to transform, but there was no other form for Cthulhu. He had no human form.

As expected, it was for naught, and Cthulhu's eyes glowed. Bastian began to scream and thrash, clawing at his own face. After another moment, Cthulhu disintegrated Bastian.

"I thought I'd raised him properly, but clearly, I was mistaken. I won't do so in the future. You, you are free to go," he said.

"Thank you," I replied weakly, glad he was able to communicate mentally.

The elders swam out, bowed to Cthulhu as he swam away, and then looked over at me.

"You have thirty minutes to leave," the woman informed me. "If you're still here after that time, I will kill you."

I dipped my head to let her know I understood, not wanting to waste any energy on speaking.

For fifteen minutes, I rested on the sea floor, letting my body recuperate enough so I could leave.

A small blowfish swam towards me, casting nervous glances about before darting over and transforming into an adorable female toddler. "Here," she whispered and shoved a seaweed-wrapped object into my mouth.

Chewing revealed it to be a clam that had been imbued with healing energy. After chewing it up, at least half of my magic and energy returned.

"Thank you," I whispered, casting my gaze to the side to avoid looking at her.

"You saved us," she whispered. "The meanies on the council won't admit it, but I saw it. I don't have much, but wanted to give you something to help you get home."

Home. What was home anymore?

"Thank you," she repeated.

"Thank you for caring," I replied and smiled.

She returned my smile, shifted back into her blowfish form, and swam quickly to the nearest buildings.

Casting one last glance at my birthplace, I shifted forms and swam away.

38

The further I got from Atlantis, the deeper my sorrow grew.

Again ... once again I had been cast out, cast aside.

Was this my destiny? Was I always to be cast away? Forever alone?

Mindlessly, I swam. The tides took me where they wanted. I had no pull, no true north. Nothing I was guided towards.

Now that I'd officially been banned, there was no longer a pull towards Atlantis. That just increased my depression.

My chest ached, and then a warmth began to build.

What was it? What was this warmth I felt?

I was about to ignore it when I felt it building, becoming an inferno as I continued to swim.

The warmth began to chase away the chill I felt in my bones ... in my soul.

I swam faster, hurrying towards the source of the warmth.

Ahead, a light bobbed in the water. It was a cool orange color and drew me towards it.

Part of me worried it was a giant, magical angler fish. One had almost eaten me when I was young and drifted too low.

"Kass!" Jong-min yelled in my mind.

The light dissipated to reveal the foursome in a bubble of air seated upon a wooden pallet, pulled by Cap'n Two-Teeth in full shark form, his hat still atop his head.

My mind refused to accept the scene before me, so I swam around them in a circle to try to comprehend it.

Jong-min, Jong-hyun, Grant, and Reed sat within a bubble of air on a half-rotted wooden pallet, a rope from the board going through the bubble and to the hook stuck in Cap'n Two-Teeth's dorsal fin.

"Surface," Jong-min ordered. His voice was somewhat muffled by the bubble and the water around us, but I made out that one word.

Still trying to process the insanity of what I was seeing, I obeyed, following Cap'n Two-Teeth to the surface, where we both shifted forms, me into full human form while Cap stayed in the half-shift form I normally saw him in. The bubble popped around the guys, disappearing.

"What?" I gaped.

Grant and Reed each grabbed one of my wrists and pulled me up onto the board, wrapping me in a hug.

"I knew you were okay," Grant whispered.

"Fuck," Reed whispered as he clung to me.

Their warmth surrounded me, and I relaxed in their hold, trying to hold back the emotions from my recent battle and banishment.

Jong-min and Jong-hyun shoved Grant and Reed aside to squish me between them, making a brother sandwich that I was totally hungry for.

"We've been so worried," Jong-hyun whispered in my ear.

"You shouldn't have run off like that," Jong-min growled.

Was it my imagination or were they ... purring?

"We should get back to shore. You four wouldn't last long out here," Cap'n Two-Teeth said as he cast his gaze around us.

"What was your plan?" I asked and stepped out of the brothers' hold. "If someone had popped that bubble while you were far below the surface, you would have drowned."

"I tried to warn them," Cap'n Two-Teeth said.

Turning, I narrowed my eyes at him. "Yet, you brought them all the way out here."

He looked down a moment before meeting my gaze with his one eye and said, "We were all worried about ya. Life ain't the same when you ain't there."

I hugged him, mindful of the hook in his dorsal fin. "Thank you for caring."

"Cap is right," Grant said. "We should return to the shore, so we can talk on solid ground."

"Can you recreate that bubble?" I asked.

Jong-min and Jong-hyun nodded and replied simultaneously, "Yes."

Cap and I shifted into our full shark forms and circled the floating pallet.

My heart felt warmer as we swam back towards the city.

The only concern I had now was facing Theo.

39

"You insufferable, inconsiderate, beautiful bitch!" Theo yelled as she stomped towards me on the beach, tears in her eyes and fists clenched at her sides.

I threw my arms around her and squeezed as tightly as I could without bruising her human body. "I'm sorry."

Tears leaked down her face, and she sobbed softly as she clung to me. "I thought you were dead."

"I'll never be able to apologize enough," I whispered.

Silver stood just behind her with his arms crossed over his chest. His scowl was enough to make me second guess our standing.

"What happened?" Theo asked, once she finally let me go.

"It's a long story. Can we go somewhere more comfortable to chat?" I made the request with no idea what they would choose. Theo had brought clothes, which I quickly put on.

"To my bar," Silver said. "It's closed right now, anyway."

It was Saturday night.

"Why is the bar closed?" I asked.

His arms flexed and he sucked in a breath. "You really think I'd be able to work while you were gone, possibly off to kill yourself?"

When I didn't reply after a moment, because yeah, I totally did think he'd be able to work no matter what I was doing, he grabbed me and pulled me into a tight hug.

"I've been sick with worry over you. Don't you ever try to sacrifice yourself like that again, you hear me? I've lived a long life, and if anyone should be sacrificing themselves, it's me. You've got so much life left to live. So many things left to experience."

"I'm sorry." Tears spilled silently down my cheeks as he hugged me. He was the closest thing to a father that I had.

"Let's go," Jong-min said, interrupting our moment. "I want to hear everything."

Wiping my face, I moved to walk beside Theo, but Grant and Reed stepped in the way and took each of my hands.

I wanted to comment, but it was nice to have their warmth, their touch, and their attention.

"So, what have you guys been up to while I've been gone for ... how many days have I been gone?"

"Two weeks," Reed growled.

I stopped walking, causing our whole procession to come to an abrupt halt.

"Two ... weeks?" I asked.

Grant nodded. "Yes. That's why we came after you."

How could it have possibly been that long? I hadn't felt like that many days had passed.

"Come on," Theo said, squeezing between Grant and me

to take my arm, and pulled me up the beach. "We are all anxiously waiting to hear Kass's tale."

Two weeks. It didn't seem possible.

We reached Silver's bar, and a sense of sadness draped over me like a blanket over my head.

The doors were closed, there were no people waiting in line, and Tonka did not stand outside.

Silver unlocked the door with a key and pushed it open. "Please enter and relax."

As soon as I stepped inside, Zara and Zyra ambushed me.

They took turns squeezing me so tightly, I was worried I'd bruise.

Zara sniffled, but held her tears in. "I'm so glad you're home."

"If you do something so stupid again, Fishling, I will cut your legs off," Zyra threatened.

I kissed her cheek and smiled. "I love you, too, sister."

She sniffled, but quickly covered it up by growling and punching my arm.

"Let's push some tables together, so we can all sit and talk," Silver suggested.

Jong-hyun and Jong-min helped Zyra and Zara push the tables together, all four smiling at each other.

A sense of dread filled my stomach.

Had the twins fallen for each other? Had I lost my chance with them by going on this suicide mission?

I expected some fallout and backlash, but losing the feline shifter twins to the troll twins would be a huge blow. One I wasn't sure I could accept by staying in the same town as them. No, I didn't love the twins, but I was startled to realize the depth of my feelings towards them. I had grown attached to them.

"Baby, you're here, on solid ground, and safe," Grant whispered to me.

I jerked my head up and realized I had been glaring at the ground, without speaking to any of them, and had no idea for how long since everyone but Grant and I were seated.

Quickly, I took the seat at the head of the table and cleared my throat. "I know you all have a lot of opinions about what I did, and will have even more about what happened, but please just hold in your comments until I finish telling you the story. Okay?"

There were a few growls, but everyone nodded in agreement.

With a deep breath for courage, I began the story, starting from the beginning when he had captured me as a teenager, tortured me, siphoned my magic, to when I had been saved by a very powerful sea witch, able to run away due to her sacrifice.

I wished I could change my past, save *her* instead of her rescuing me, but life was like that sometimes. Sometimes you had to accept the chaos that had happened and acknowledge there was no way to repair it, no way to undo what had been done.

"He decided there was no point in sending his minions to capture me when he'd drained so much of my magic already. I drifted through the seas, just surviving, which was harder at other times when pods attacked me. Theo found me and rescued me sometime after that, when I washed up on the shore here. So, let's fast forward to Bastian returning."

I took a long drink before continuing.

"Bastian found out from his minions' spying and asking around that Theo and I were friends, and that Silver and I cared for each other. So, he kidnapped them to try to use them as a bait. It worked. Even though I freed you, he would have just recaptured you." I looked up at Zara and Zyra. "Or you two. He would have found people I cared about to force me back. I don't deserve you all as it is, and there is no way I could ever sacrifice you for myself. Plus, this was part of my backstory, not yours. We left here and headed towards Atlantis, yes, *the* Atlantis. That's where I'm from, where I was born and raised for several years before we were banished. My banishment was not something I remembered.

"Bastian had a seal shifter who could make you hallucinate or dream or something. She made me believe we had reached Atlantis, and I faced the Council there. She made me remember the memories I had blocked. Memories that showed I had been banished and my parents, not wanting to send such a young child out on their own, followed me into banishment."

"Why were you banished?" Silver asked.

This was something I wasn't certain how the guys would take. Would they stop dating me if they found out? Not that we had dated that long, anyway. There was nothing to do but rip the Band-Aid off in one yank.

"I have the ability to stop shifters from shifting," I answered.

40

"All shifters, or just aquatic shifters?" Theo asked.

That made me pause.

"I'm not certain," I admitted. "However, that's why the Atlanteans banished me. Because I made them weak."

"Weak? That's a huge advantage if you learned how to control it and harnessed it against your enemies," Grant said.

His comment surprised me. That hadn't been something I had considered, but then again, I'd not known about my magic, and just thought about it as a curse.

"You're not a curse," Reed whispered. "Your magic is not a curse. I know that's what the Council told you, what you've felt, but every magic can be used in a positive way."

Blinking away tears and shoving all the emotions back into their boxes, I looked back up at them. "We finally made it to the real Atlantis, and I had to pretend to be on Bastian's side. Luckily, I was able to pretend that one of the councilors had the power to compel me to leave, giving them the ability to shift again and giving me time to kill a couple of Bastian's minions."

The taste of seal girl's flesh filled me, and I had to swallow some excess drool.

"What did you eat?" Theo asked with a smirk.

"Just a bite!" I shouted.

"Seal is delicious," Zyra said with a wide smile.

Zara's nose scrunched. "Better when cooked."

"Girls," Silver snapped.

"Sorry, Dad," Zyra, Zara, Theo, and I replied at the same time.

"So, I killed a couple and then ... " I paused and took a deep breath. "Cthulhu showed up."

"What?" everyone screeched.

"Apparently, he had raised Bastian, and Bastian was trying to amass enough power to defeat him. Bastian tried to take me hostage ..."

Silver, Reed, Grant, Jong-min, and Jong-hyun growled.

"... but Cthulhu made him release me and let me go free. The Council banished me again." I remembered the little girl and her kindness, and smiled. Maybe all of the Atlanteans weren't awful.

"Then what?" Silver asked.

I shrugged. "I was pretty magically depleted, so I drifted, headed this way, but in a daze. The foursome here showed up with Cap'n Two-Teeth and brought me all the way back. And that ... that's my tale."

"You're always involved in the craziest events," Theo said softly. "I definitely picked the most interesting woman to be my bestie."

"Aw, you're so sweet," I said and winked at her.

"So, now what?" Reed asked.

I scowled. "Huh?"

"What are your plans now?" Silver asked.

My brow furrowed further as I looked at them. "Um, see if I still have a job at the aquarium and still have a place to live. Return to life as normal ... or as normal as my life has ever been."

Someone knocked on the door to the bar.

Everyone stood.

Zyra pulled a sword.

Grant and Reed partially shifted.

Theo had magic gathered in her palm.

Silver stood, walked to the door, and opened it.

The tension was palpable.

"We wish to speak to the shark shifter," a somewhat familiar male voice said.

Where did I know him from?

I wracked my brain, trying to remember, but couldn't. Definitely not someone I dated. Was it someone I scammed?

That would definitely be my luck.

Was it one of the tiger shifters?

"You attack anyone, and I revoke my hospitality," Silver grumbled as he stepped back.

As he opened the door, the hunter who'd given me his card stepped inside. He dipped his head.

"He's dead," I said. "Cthulhu killed him."

"Cthulhu?" he asked.

"Apparently, he raised him, and Bastian was trying to gain the power to defeat Cthulhu."

The hunter snorted. "Serves him right for being so delusional."

"Is that all you came here for?" I asked.

He glanced down a second, with an almost bashful

expression, before looking back up at me. "I, uh, also wanted to check to see how you were doing."

My brows furrowed. "Wait, how did you know I was back?"

"How *did* you know?" Grant asked as he stepped forward, fists clenched.

"I've been watching Silver's, waiting for her to return," he answered, though it seemed like a partial truth based on the red blooming on his cheeks.

Wait ... was he interested in me?

No.

What?

No way.

"Look, I just recapped everything, and don't really feel like doing it again right now. I've been on land for like ... an hour, so I need some time to recuperate and readjust to being here."

"I understand," he said with a nod. He held out a business card and said, "Call me when you are free and ready to talk. I'm glad you're back and safe."

One of the feline shifter twins growled softly, but I wasn't sure which one, or if anyone else had heard it.

"Thank you. I will," I promised.

He smiled, nodded to Silver, and left.

"You withholding whore!" Theo whisper-hissed.

"No," I said, tucked the card in my pocket, and shook my head. "Not what you think."

Theo just scoffed, gave a pointed glance at the angry guys still standing and glaring at the closed door, and said, "Sure it's not."

"Catch me up on what's happened since I left." I plopped down in my seat and drained the second half of my drink.

Silver took the glass out of my hand, walked up to the bar, and started making me a new drink.

"Well, aside from a lot of cursing, drinking, moping, and destruction ... not much," Zara said.

"Zara," Silver growled.

"She's right," Zyra said. "I destroyed several tables and killed a few people. Dad destroyed an entire building. Theo and the boys wiped out a vampire clan. Zara ... well, she didn't destroy anything as that's not her style."

"I cast a lot of spells trying to force you to return home," Zara admitted.

My eyes snapped to Theo. "You wiped out a vamp clan?"

She flinched. "Maybe."

"Please tell me you did not just start a war because you were mad at me," I whispered. There were a few vampires I could think of her wanting to kill, but I hesitated in asking.

Silver set my drink in front of me and said, "Hard to start a war when your entire clan is gone."

Oh, jellyfish.

My chin dropped forward, I shook my head, and then the hilarity of the situation had me laughing so hard that my entire body quaked. I threw my head back as I continued to laugh.

Laughing that much had me with tears that streamed down my face. Those tears turned into true, body wracking sobs.

Why? Why were all these wonderful, amazing, and beautiful people in my life? Why did they care about me? Love me?

"I don't deserve you ... any of you," I sobbed, the words broken apart by my gasping breaths.

Theo, Zara, and Zyra pulled me up out of my chair to wrap me up in a group hug. We'd had these group hugs, with various of us in the middle, many times over the last several years.

"You are worthy of love," Zara whispered as she nuzzled me, careful to keep her tusks away from Theo.

Zyra tightened her grip on me. "We will always love you, fishling."

"We have to love you enough to compensate for you not loving yourself," Theo said.

"If only I were gay," I chuckled and wiped at my eyes.

The three women around me laughed and relaxed their holds.

"You're too chaotic for me," Zara teased.

"Much too thin," Zyra said.

"Too short and full of drama," Theo said, and flipped her hair over her shoulder.

"I appreciate you humbling me so." I knew they were just teasing me, and their teasing made me so much happier.

"Will you come with us tonight?" Grant asked suddenly.

Zara, Zyra, Theo, and I turned as one to look at him.

"Come with you?" I asked.

41

"Will you come back to our place, so we can speak to you?" he clarified.

With a wide smile, I walked up to him until I had to tilt my head back to look up at him. "I supposed I should give the four men who ventured out into the open ocean to find me at least an evening of my time."

"I still can't believe you guys did that without consulting me." Theo crossed her arms and stuck her lip out in a huge pout.

Stepping back, I bowed to the group. "Thank you, for caring about me, and for being here for me now. I meant it when I said I didn't deserve you all. I will never be able to apologize enough or make it up to you, but I hope we can all continue on and move forward."

"I have to go to sleep, because I have work tomorrow," Theo said. "Meet me after work, so we can come by Silver's?"

I looked at Silver. "Am I still welcome here?"

He sighed and shook his head. "As if I could keep you away."

"You'll always be welcome here," Zara and Zyra said simultaneously.

"We have food and snacks at the house," Reed said with a smile. "Plenty to satiate the hunger I can hear from your stomach."

House? Had they purchased something, or just moved to a rental house instead of the apartment?

"We will see you tomorrow," Zyra said. "If you don't come, I will hunt you down."

I kissed her cheek. "Love you, sister."

She sniffled and looked away.

Jong-min held open the door of the bar and waited for me to exit before closing it.

The four of them encircled me as we walked, and a weird ache formed in my chest.

"So, you two seemed close to Zara and Zyra," I commented to Jong-hyun.

"We spent a lot of time with that group over the past week," he replied immediately.

"They're great women," I said with a soft smile.

"Zyra killed that orca pod who kept harassing you," Jong-min said. "We barely contained her rage enough not to kill a pod of dolphins who walked in right after."

My eyes felt like they had bulged out of my skull. "What!"

"Silver wasn't even upset," Jong-hyun added.

Grant scoffed. "He spit on their leader's body before calling for it to be cleaned up."

What in the name of Poseidon's Trident had happened?

"Was there a rogue mage in town? Clearly someone cast

a spell on you all." I muttered the words, but they all heard them.

They didn't speak the rest of the walk, surprising me when they walked into the closest suburban neighborhood, and into a three-story house with a metal fence that had small gargoyle statues on it.

I paused at the gargoyles, narrowed my eyes, and asked, "How'd you bribe the babies to stay here and guard your place?"

"We saved them from the vampires, and they didn't have a home to return to. So, they live here now," Grant explained.

My mouth dropped and I stared, dumbfounded, at the men before me. They'd adopted a trio of gargoyle kids?

"Let's get inside." Jong-min's words were clipped, and he pushed his hand against my lower back to propel me through the gate and up the steps to their house.

Jong-hyun removed the wards and stepped back. "Please enter our home and make yourself comfortable."

Passing by him, I kissed his cheek, before continuing inside the foyer. I let out a whistle as I looked at the pristine place. "How much are you renting this place for? It's beautiful."

"We aren't renting it," Reed said.

The four walked by me, turned down a hallway, and I heard pots and plates being moved.

Hurrying to follow after them, I found them in a state-of-the-art kitchen with chrome everything.

"What do you mean you aren't renting it?"

Reed held out a cookie to me while smiling softly. "We told you that we've been searching for a place to call our own."

Grant pulled some vegetables out of the fridge and set them on the counter. "We've been here long enough that we decided this is a great place to be our new home."

After a gulp, I asked, "So, you're going to be in town for … a while then?" I was trying not to get my hopes up.

The four nodded simultaneously, while all taking part in the preparation of some meal.

Instead of asking more questions that they didn't seem to want to elaborate on right now, I ate the cookie Reed had given me. As soon as I took the first bite, I realized how starving I was and shoved the entire thing into my mouth.

"We'll give you a tour after we eat," Jong-hyun said. He expertly fried some bell peppers and onions in a pan, flipping them with just a flick of his wrist and no spatula in sight.

Jong-min cooked some noodles in a pot, scowling as he did so.

"What did the noodles do to earn that scowl? I was fairly certain you reserved that level of brow furrowing for me only." The teasing was natural and felt good to be able to do with him.

"I prefer fresh noodles," he muttered. "These ones don't have the right consistency, no matter how I cook them."

He hadn't risen to my bait. Damn.

"Can I do anything?" I asked.

"Just stay there," Reed whispered. "Just … don't leave."

The way his voice broke at the end made me flinch and had all of the bravado I'd been mustering leave me in a rush.

Taking a step back, so I could lean against the counters, I crossed my arms over my stomach and hugged myself.

Leaving them had hurt, but I'd done it to protect them. To keep them all safe.

I couldn't blame them for being mad at me, though. In their shoes, I'd have been pissed, too.

The food was quickly finished, plated, and they gathered the plates in their hands.

"Come on," Grant coaxed. "Let's go sit and eat."

After nodding and pushing off from the counter, I followed him down the hall and to a large dining room. They had a long dining table with about a dozen chairs around it.

"This is a huge dining room," I commented, as I sat in the chair Grant pulled out for me—the head of the table, I belatedly noticed.

"That's what she said," Reed replied with a chuckle.

I rolled my eyes and looked at the plate of food before me. "It smells delicious." Before they could make a comment, I took a bite and immediately moaned. "Tastes amazing, too."

The silence while we ate wouldn't have been uncomfortable normally, but their hunched shoulders, frowns, and occasional sad puppy eyes were a bit unnerving.

Finally done eating, we all carried our plates to the kitchen and then headed to a living room with three couches.

I chose one of the smallest couches, hoping to cuddle up next to one of them, but they took the other two couches, instead. Nerves built and my palms began to sweat. I rubbed them on my jeans and fidgeted in my seat. What was happening? Was this an intervention?

"I know I haven't been the most welcoming person to you," Jong-min said. "It's because I've been hurt before, and I didn't want to get to know you, to like you, if we were just going to part ways."

I shrugged one shoulder and smiled. "I assumed your

prickly nature was because of your overprotectiveness of your brother and friends."

"That was part of it," he admitted with a nod.

"See? You understand us, you get us," Reed said. "You immediately fit in with each of us and us as a group. That's why you came over to watch a movie."

"I'm chaos," I said. "Don't you remember the first time you met me, Jong-min? You almost attacked me when I walked into the hotel. I bit a girl's arm off right in front of you and was seriously considering eating the other people in the bar with us, Grant."

"It was *so* hot," he moaned and smiled wide.

"I'm aquatic," I reminded them.

They all shrugged.

"There are always compromises and things you have to accept about the other person. There are always struggles in relationships, but there comes a point where you realize that those little things don't matter. What matters is being together and spending the rest of your lives together," Jong-hyun said.

"What are you guys saying?" I blurted with wide eyes. "Are ... are ..." I didn't dare voice my thought, my hope.

Grant slid off the couch he sat on to kneel before me. "We missed you more than anything in this world, Kassidy. We've never missed someone as much as we missed you. Only the knowledge that you weren't dead kept us going. Gave us hope that you would return to us."

"How did you know I was alive?" The words were barely a whisper because I was fairly certain I already knew. That night Grant, Reed, and I had slept together, something had happened between us ... something magical. And I didn't just mean the sex.

He smiled softly. "You know."

"Say it," I whispered. "I have to hear you say it, so I know I'm not imagining things. That my desires aren't becoming hallucinations." That I'm not so far gone, so starved for love that I'm seeing shit that isn't there.

"We have a connection, a magical one. It's not supposed to happen until the official binding ceremony, but nothing about you, or us, is normal. All that is required is an agreement, and it seems we just needed a mental one. It's not a full mating bond yet, but it's there."

Looking with just my eyes at Jong-min, I saw him scowl and touch his chest.

"Us. All of us," he whispered and raised his head to look at me. "We have it, too."

"That's why we were able to heal her so well and break Bastian's hold," Jong-hyun said, his mouth fell open and he stared at me, dumbfounded.

Grant rested his hand on my knee, drawing my attention back to him. "We've always known we would share a woman, ever since we formed our pack. We share a connection between the four of us already, one that cannot be broken, except in death. The connection we have with you isn't permanent, yet, so don't freak out just yet about it.

"We know there is a lot of your past we need to learn about, more so than what you discussed earlier today in the bar. We haven't shared our pasts with you, and we want to rectify that. Before we do, though, we want to ask you: will you allow the four of us to court you?"

42

If I was the fainting type, I would have fainted right then and there.

"You're serious?" I asked. "The four of you, the four males in front of me, you four, you all want to court me with the intention of becoming my permanent, lifelong mates?"

I was hallucinating.

That fucking seal bitch was alive, and this was a hallucination she was forcing me to see.

Tilting my head, I looked for any flicker, waver, or indication that it was her hallucination.

Nothing.

Standing, I marched towards the front door, but Grant and Reed each grabbed one of my wrists.

"We're serious. Yes," Reed said immediately.

"Yes, that is our intention," Grant blurted.

"This has to be a hallucination. I'm in Atlantis and the seal bitch is messing with me. That has to be it. This ... this can't be real." The words were a whisper, but the pain I felt at the hope it was real was so intense, I could hardly breathe.

Grant turned me sideways and his lips crashed into mine in a fiercely passionate and fiery kiss. I stepped closer, letting his body heat warm me, grabbed a handful of hair, and pulled him down to deepen the kiss.

He pulled back after a moment, panting and smiling. "Still think it's a hallucination?"

I touched my swollen lips. "If it is, I'm okay with it."

His smile turned smug and he kissed my cheek. "Come sit down, please?"

Reed still had hold of my right wrist, and when I turned to look at him, I saw that the kiss with Grant had definitely excited him.

He stared at my lips a moment, licked his, and then blinked. The blink brought him back to the present, and he released me to walk back to the couches.

After sitting back down, I took a deep breath and asked, "How are we doing this?"

Grant smiled. "Well, that's really up to you, but we were hoping ..." He glanced at the twins, who nodded simultaneously and then at Reed who also nodded. "... we were hoping you might come and live with us, here."

It was always better to live together with someone before you got too serious. Living together let you see all their habits and was essential, in my opinion, for determining whether you were actually a match or not.

This house was actually really centrally located to the aquarium, Silver's bar, and Theo's. I could walk to them all within half an hour max. It would also be nice to have a dresser of my own in a room of my own, too. Wait, would I have my own room?

"Would I have my own room?" I asked hopefully.

Grant nodded. "Of course."

Jong-min scoffed. "Duh."

"Nope, you have to share with one of us each night," Reed said with a wink.

"Wait, I retract my answer," Grant said quickly.

I laughed softly and shook my head. These men were something else.

"Okay, so I'll move in, but I'm still working at the aquarium. I can't disappoint the kids by making them think they won't see me anymore." I paused and my chin dropped forward. "Well, that is if I still have a job."

"I'm sure they'd love to have you back. They probably just told people that you were sick and not on display while you were recuperating. If anything, they'd say they released you to the wild," Jong-hyun said.

"I'll need to get my things from Theo's place," I said.

Reed rubbed the back of his neck while smiling sheepishly. "Actually, I kind of got your stuff from her already. She was pretty certain you would agree to move in with us, and said we could blame her if you got mad."

That definitely sounded like Theo. My best friend loved to meddle, and had been trying to find me a man to love since we'd started going out to bars together.

"Can I get that tour now?" I asked with a smile.

Thank you for reading. I hope you enjoyed this first season of SHARK.

For more paranormal reverse harem romance with sexy shifters check out the completed series **Her Royal Harem** available in Kindle Unlimited, audiobook, and paperback.

Join my newsletter to stay up to date on releases, sales, and freebies: catbanks.co/newsletter